THE
INVISIBLE
GIRL

CW01456503

CL FARLEY

LUNA NOVELLA #19

Luna Press PUBLISHING

Text Copyright © 2024 Caitlin Lyle Farley
Cover © 2024 Jay Johnstone

First published by Luna Press Publishing, Edinburgh, 2024

The right of Caitlin Lyle Farley to be identified as the Author of the Work has been asserted by her in accordance with the Copyright, Designs and Patents Act 1988.

The Invisible Girl ©2024. All rights reserved. No part of this publication may be reproduced, stored in a retrieval system, or transmitted in any form or by any means, electronic, mechanical, photocopy, recording or otherwise, without prior written permission of the copyright owners. Nor can it be circulated in any form of binding or cover other than that in which it is published and without similar condition including this condition being imposed on a subsequent purchaser.

www.lunapresspublishing.com
ISBN-13: 978-1-915556-22-6

For every square peg trying to fit
into society's round holes.

Contents

The Melting Point of Glass

why are there cracks?

Maggie lifted her hand until her fingers aligned with the cracks in the sky. She traced the bloody fissures across the blue, her fingers travelling into the last light of day while her feet followed. Only the fence bordering the vegetable patch stopped her from chasing the sunset into its eventual death. *drama queen*

She gripped the wire mesh keeping her caged in life; an unfair oversight when so many others had died to the Shadows, died in her hands.

"You're dawdling, girl."

"Eya, Mme," Maggie replied.

"The marog isn't going to harvest itself and I still want to eat tonight."

"It won't take long." Maggie turned to Puleng, who sat on a large rock near the middle of the garden. Her hair was neatly trimmed and brushed out, and she definitely wasn't dead even if Puleng's lips were red like warning lights. *how odd?*

Sometimes Maggie dreamed about how different the earth smelled when you dug deep enough, and Puleng's sheet-wrapped body—fragile as a bunch of sticks—exploding into a flock of Mercurochrome red weaver birds when the first spadeful of dirt landed on her chest. But a slippery wrongness

Why Maggie do you worry people are dead or not around you?

lived in the memory. It had something to do with the picture quality on the TV the catfish spat out for Maggie while she was drowning. If Puleng had died, then who had held her tight and stroked her hair during that first night after she was exiled from the zoo? Who was watching her now with pursed lips and tapping fingers?

Maggie frowned against the wall her thoughts had run into. Ideas didn't used to be this wormy but her brain was all boxes and water slides now. Navigation was a hand finding a wall in the dark. She was giving herself a headache.

Puleng shook her head and said something in Sesotho, too quick and low for Maggie to hear. She turned back to the sunset, to the light, and the monsters roaming the veld beyond the fence.

Creepy

The creatures were chimeras of mismatched animal parts elongated to weird proportions by the sinking sun, children of light skinned with shadows and fear. One of them stalked wobbly circles on a boulder that rose above the tall yellow grass. Its back half resembled a leopard, the front half an African wild dog, and the massive tusks sprouting from its head were straight off an elephant. The position of the tusks was misleading, a trickery that brought to mind the massive horns of those cattle Uncle Cyril owned in the time before the shadows, but Maggie wasn't fooled. The curve and tapering of the tusks made their truth obvious.

The shadow's limbs stretched like chewing gum as the light faded further, its steps growing more uncertain until it collapsed. The remains oozed down the side of the boulder to nestle in the womb of deeper darkness at its base. Light's children died when she did. Once, Maggie would've welcomed the night. She would've released her invisibility power and relaxed, but now, she rarely let down the shield that hid her from the world.   *Show us your superpower*

"Girl, can you hear my stomach grumbling?"

"No, Mme."

"It's like a pack of wild dogs. They want to bite your nose off."

Maggie chuckled. "Only my nose?

"It is a Pinocchio nose," Puleng made a quiet, disapproving sound, "and it's become very long from your lies about hurrying with the food."

No, Puleng hadn't died. That was just another illusion Arno had inflicted on her the day he attacked her mind. Nevertheless, the guilt that lie had embedded in her chest was real. The pointed tip of it emerged near the bottom of her collarbone, something often felt but rarely seen.

"I'm doing it now, Mme." Maggie left the fence and went back to kneel among the untidy clumps of wild spinach.

"And you should've been doing it just now already."

Maggie sighed and lifted the knife she'd brought to cut the leaves.

"You must find something nice to feed those chickens, girl," Puleng said. "They haven't been giving eggs."

"There's probably beetle grubs in the compost pile."

"Then you must dig them out. Some worms too."

"There's no way I'm giving them any of my worms!"

"Who do you think you're talking to?"

Maggie peered at Puleng and withered in her glare. "Sorry, Mme."

Puleng sucked her teeth and primly crossed her legs. "This girl!"

Maggie ducked her head. Mme Puleng hadn't been exiled.

She'd chosen to follow Maggie out here to a lonely house edged by the Seven Dams nature reserve and the Bloemfontein Botanical gardens so she wouldn't be alone. Maggie had vowed she'd show her appreciation by never speaking back to Puleng, or arguing with her, or being anything less than good and dutiful, but it was difficult to maintain.

Maggie gathered the greens and they left the garden as the jackals started singing in the low hills to the north-east. She let Puleng walk ahead of her on the narrow dirt path curving up the slope to the pale blue house that wasn't home.

Puleng had started a fire in the pit outside the back door before joining her in the garden. The flames had settled now but the coals burned bright around the base of the cast iron pot. Maggie lifted the lid, releasing a plume of steam with a savoury scent, and threw the greens she'd gathered into the pot just as they were.

"What do you think you're doing?" Puleng shouted. "You must chop that first. How do you throw marog into the stew without chopping it, Maggie?"

Maggie opened her mouth to reply, but Puleng was still ranting.

"...not know how to cook even this basic thing?" Puleng glared at her, waiting for a response.

"But the leaves are small and you're hungry..."

The distant thrum of an engine cut her short. Maggie stared out into the pale night. A few stars twinkled in the blackness beyond the lines of clouds crossing the sky. The wan light of a sickle moon glinted vaguely on the corrugated iron rooftops of distant houses. Further off, the few tall buildings in Bloemfontein rose like blackened fangs around the faint ambient glow of light from the zoo and the nearby hotel where the other survivors lived in their solar-powered paradise. The only other light was a stark white that flickered and flashed, silhouetting pointed roofs and leafy trees in one of the suburbs that lined the far edge of the nature reserve.

"That's Enzo's bakkie," Puleng said.

Maggie nodded.

"Hey! He must be coming to take us home."

Maggie didn't answer; didn't want to be labelled a pessimist for stating obvious truths. Instead, she squatted down to tend the fire, secure in her invisibility shield.

"Eish, girl. Are you seriously going to sit here and hide when Enzo's coming to take us home?"

"Yes," Maggie replied, because even in her most vivid and realistic unrealities, home was lost to her forever.

Engine sounds travelled far in a world where the only competition came from crickets, occasional birds and the screams of animals falling prey to predators. The food was ready before the headlights from Enzo's bakkie stopped outside the gate. Maggie sat on the back step, legs stretched out toward the fire, and delivered another spoonful of bean and wild spinach stew to her mouth. The headlights cut out but the cab lit up when the driver's side door opened, reflecting off Enzo's glasses and revealing the pale, bearded stranger beside him.

Had Enzo and the others found more survivors since they exiled her? How could they, now they didn't have an invisible girl who could safely go wherever she pleased? Faizel could make electricity sing and dance, and probably use his ability to power drones too.

"Maggie!"

Enzo had stepped out of the car. He turned on a floodlight torch and Maggie shielded her eyes with one arm.

"Maggie?"

"Maybe she's out hunting?"

That had to be the stranger. His voice carried an English private school accent, like that boy Lebo brought to one of Maggie's parties, or that weird girl who played drums in Whatshisname's band. Long ago people, ghosts without relevance.

"Then what do we do? Look for the girl, or wait?"

Another voice she didn't recognise, but this one was sharp and his accent was Kaaps. Where the hell did Enzo find these people? Surely even a Faizel-powered drone couldn't fly all the way to Cape Town.

"No, she's here," Enzo sighed, "she just isn't coming out. Maggie," he raised his voice again, "please, I need to speak to you. It's important."

Maggie stood and stretched. The answer was simple: Enzo didn't find these people. Her mind was playing unrealities for her again. Dread twined through her ribs, tightening her chest. She didn't want to do this, not now or ever again. Where had Puleng gone to?

"I see your shadow, Maggie."

"So what?" she called back, already turning to go inside.

"I have to speak with you, Margaret."

That was the hoity-toity dude's voice again. It was followed by the squeak of the gate opening and hurried footsteps.

"All of our survival depends on it, depends on you," he continued, his voice drawing closer.

Maggie opened the door and kicked off her shoes. Any minute now... He groaned like sickness and slow death. The only thing about life that was constant and certain was her invisibility shield's ability to render her unseen and repulse anything that tried to get close to her. The guy with the Kaaps accent was shouting now, his voice mingling with Enzo's into a vaguely annoying buzz. They were flies on a corpse you haven't seen yet. Where was Puleng? Maggie navigated the kitchen by familiarity, striding through the darkness to switch on the portable solar battery she used to power the lights. Eishkom's loadshedding had left a useful legacy of power generating equipment in the dust and bones of middle-class houses. The LCD screen flickered on, showing it had two bars left.

"You're too stubborn, Maggie. Go speak to Enzo."

There she was. Maggie sighed and turned on the kitchen lamp. "They aren't real, Mme."

"Then how do I know Enzo is here?"

Maggie turned to study Puleng. She posed a good question, but also, she'd braided her hair flat against her scalp in the time between finishing her meal and now. Her fingers must've moved like lightning to finish the style, never mind the tiny blue flowers she'd woven into a crown over the top of her head. She was dressed to impress.

"This is real, Margaret. Real and urgent."

The man was leaning in the doorway, red-faced and sweating. She stepped toward him and he grimaced, his teeth showing white and sharp beneath a brown beard streaked with grey.

"Rob!"

"I'm fine," the man replied. He scanned the room, looking through and past her, before his gaze settled near her feet. "Margaret, please, let me speak to you."

Night was advancing and she had to make a run to one of her supply caches for more samp and tins of curry. Puleng had specifically asked her to fetch those things. It would be an onerous task if she had delusions dogging her steps all night.

But Puleng could see them. The things in her unrealities had a tendency to get worse the longer she ignored them. Puleng had even braided flowers into her hair to look nice. This Rob guy's sharp teeth implied he'd try to bite her.

"Margaret?"

"Okay, speak." Maggie lifted herself up to sit on the kitchen counter. A moment of indulgence now could prevent them chasing her later if they were false and keep Puleng happy if they were real.

Puleng cleared her throat. "Your power, Maggie. You're being so rude to leave it working."

"But it's keeping me safe," Maggie replied.

"You're already safe. Enzo wouldn't bring people here to hurt us, and I'm here."

Maggie released her shield and looked pointedly at where Puleng stood. Puleng gave her a stiff nod of approval and Maggie didn't voice any of the snarky comments that entered her mind.

"Thank you." The man visibly relaxed. He looked at her then, brow corrugated over wide eyes that scanned her like he didn't know where to look first. Maggie felt naked. Without her shield, all the spears of guilt and furry mould that infected her was on display, and there was nothing to keep him safe and distant. She should've put flowers in her hair too, and thorns.

"My name is Rob," he said. "When the Change happened—"

"The Change?"

He nodded. "The moment the shadow monsters appeared and so many of us died."

He'd given it a fancy name? What a weirdo. "Just call it the Apocalypse because that's what it was."

His hands rubbed together. "Apocalypse is a word with religious connotations that don't really fit... that's not a discussion for now, however."

"Rob! Are you okay?"

The other stranger bounded onto the back step and put a hand on Rob's shoulder. He was around her age, early twenties, with a pair of short horns growing from his forehead that curved into three symmetrical spirals. Maggie wanted to cut them off and stick them on the end of a drill so she could watch them rotating; the post-apocalyptic version of those 'Try not to be Satisfied' videos she used to watch on YouTube.

"I'm fine, Freddy." Rob waved the younger guy off, his gaze never leaving her.

"Can I have those horns when you're dead?"   LOL

Freddy also turned to look at her then, his eyes narrowing in a calculating way. Over his shoulder, Enzo's face appeared, dripping concern in fat, pus-coloured globs. Rage flared bright and hot in her veins. He looked different on the outside. The horrific wound he'd gotten when Arno attacked had become a web of pink scar tissue across the right side of his face. He'd lost his ear that night and it seemed he was using a headband to hold his glasses in place. Would the glass shatter and pierce his eyes if she hit him in the face hard enough?

"This is turning into a fucking party," Maggie muttered. Too late, she realised her mistake and turned to Puleng to apologise for swearing, but Puleng had left the room. She must've realised this was bullshit, or she'd disappeared because this was false while Puleng remained in reality.

"When the Change occurred, I gained a supernatural power, just like every other survivor," Rob said. "The thing I wanted most in that moment manifested in reality."

It was both freeing and frightening to be without Puleng. She missed her already, but with her absent, Maggie could say or do whatever she pleased to these freaks.

"My power is clairvoyance," Rob continued. "The ability to see the future."

Maggie snorted. "And how'd you get a power like that? Were you watching the stock market?"

He's such "No, I was looking for someone, but that's beside the point. a For almost a year now I've been having visions of a person with a power that can defeat the origin of the shadow monsters, the You are being who caused the Change." He leaned towards her. "That the person is you, Margaret."

chosen one"

Maggie hopped down from the counter. Shards of green and clear glass with jagged edges erupted from the linoleum when her feet made contact with the floor.

"So, you're here because you want me to save the world?" She began to pace, watching as more glass emerged with every step she took, rippling outwards across the floor in miniature shock waves. "I have no reason to fight the shadows. As long as I'm wearing my shield, they leave me alone. Everything does."

"Not everyone has that advantage."

"That's not my problem." She tipped her head to watch a reflection caught in one of the larger glass shards around her feet. It was a face, but it was gone before she recognised who it belonged to.

"Maggie, please. Be reasonable." Enzo sounded like he might cry. "I know I have no right to ask you this, but we need you. You can destroy the shadows with your power. You can ensure Bibi grows up in a world where she can go outside in the day and prevent anyone else dying like Sam did."

The laughter burst from Maggie so hard that she had to

lean against the kitchen counter. Oh, this was weird. Weird, weird, weird, but it was good because it was so obviously ridiculous. If she could see the stitches then she knew where the seams were. If she knew where the seams and the stitches were then she could find the knots that kept them secure. The wounds beneath would breathe then, and cease to ooze, and there would be no more unreality.   *this author oversed worked her*

"Enzo wouldn't say that to me." She <u>vomited the</u> words *sentences* out between gasps that might've been sobs if she'd troubled to catch one and dissect it—the knives were sharp and just within reach since she and Puleng used this counter for butchering chickens, rabbits and pigeons after they'd cleaned the small carcasses. "Enzo would know that I'd never help him after what he did to me."

"What about the rest of the world?"

She looked up at Rob. He'd entered the house uninvited and was surfing toward her, borne on a wave of broken glass.

"We've done nothing to you," he gestured to himself and Freddy. "Would you let everyone else who survived the Change continue to suffer because others harmed you?"

"Sure." Maggie shrugged. "What a pointless question. What do I care about the rest of the world?

Rob paused. "You could end this, Margaret, end all the fear and uncertainty the shadows cause. We could start rebuilding the world."

It would be nice to have internet again, and TikTok, but the rest of it? Well, it was probably a great place for private-schooled old white dudes like Rob.

"There are other groups of survivors out there. Freddy and I met them on our journey to Bloemfontein. If we all could travel safely by day then we could start working together to

CL Farley

fucking idealist

rebuild infrastructure, share our abilities to help each other rebuild—"

"It's looping now, isn't it?" She shook her head. "But I'm still not going to agree."

"And why the fuck not?" Freddy stomped forward to stand across from her on the other side of the counter. "Are you such an asshole that you'd refuse to help what could be thousands of people just because, like, twenty of them hurt your feelings?"

"They kicked me out of my home when I was injured, when I needed them most," she snarled at him. "They couldn't handle what happened to me, how I changed because of what Arno did, so they threw me away."

"That's not true, Maggie, you were hurting people—"

"Shut up!" She jabbed her finger at Enzo. "You have no idea what it's like to be trapped in your own head, to be tortured... you never even tried to understand what I was going through."

"I did, I tried as hard as I could." Enzo's lip quivered and his face wrinkled. His purulent concern oozed along the furrows. "Arno attacked us too when we found you."

"Shut up," she muttered, turning back to Freddy. "Nothing changes the past, therefore nothing changes in the now. I ain't doing shit for you."

Maggie eyed the sharp tips of his horns and watched the black of his pupils swirl into an incandescent red. Was the violence starting?

"What are you going to do about it?" she asked. The safety of her shield was just around her shoulders, waiting to be pulled tight. It might be easier to fight and kill and be done with this.

He opened his mouth to answer, but Rob had joined him and put a hand on his shoulder.

Why is this so predictable!

"We will do everything we can to change your mind, Margaret. We'll camp on your doorstep if that's what it takes."

Maggie pulled the sharpest knife from the knife block. "I am not going to be haunted by make-believe men selling fantasies about saving the world."

"Don't!"

Enzo had moved forward, but he quickly backed away with his hands raised when she pointed the knife at him.

"You want to go first?" Maggie moved towards him.

"Maggie, we're really here. This isn't a psychotic episode. We're real." Enzo's eyes were wide and his voice tinny with fear. The palms of his hands were swelling. The bulges turned white, skin cells dying and turning to flakes which wove themselves into threads. Egg sacs... he'd brought some nasty bug babies with him.

"That's what they always say. They're always real when they want you to believe them and always gone when I need them."

She stepped past the edge of the counter and then a hand closed around her wrist. The world spun two and a half times and, when it stopped again, she was being restrained. Arms like cable ties holding her, touching, touching, fingers digging *very sensory* into her wrist to strum on her tendons and they sang, so sweetly. Sweat like diamonds glistening, sliding, smelling like the hot, closed spaces where limbs joined torso, and the dirt hiding under fallen leaves. Touching, touching, crawling over her skin. Words hot on her neck and Rob and Enzo both were melting like oil paintings. Their colours smeared together to shape shoulders and a head behind them, a blurry silhouette that made her skin crawl with familiarity.

"This was the moment when Maggie realised she'd never left the island," the narrator said. He was still blurry but

wtf where did you come from?

his colours were separating into clothes and skin, lines and shadow. A hood covered his face.

"What?" Maggie wailed. "That can't be true!"

"But it is."

The man sidled between the smudged forms of Enzo and Rob, bumping them both. Their heads snapped loose and floated away, revolving through the air with mouths open, fangs gleaming.

"You're still here, Maggie, with me." The man cupped her chin and now she saw Arno's small, too-blue eyes and sharp nose beneath the shadow of his hood; the blissful, thin-lipped smile and the joyful tears laying tracks down his cheeks.

"You will always be here with me."

Was it all another episode of Arno's Catfish TV? A second season flashback to what came before, when Arno lost his mind first and tried to take hers with him, except before was still now and after never happened. Was Arno the villain who faked his own death to return later in the series?

But that was the narrator's voice, not Arno's. And his hands... too smooth when they slid from her chin to cup her cheeks. The narrator might look like Arno, but he was a cheap copy, a try-hard who skipped over the finer details. She noticed it just before her face went numb, succumbing to the tingling ice spreading through her body. It was false. It had to be because the water in Loch Logan wasn't this cold and the catfish weren't here. There was no 'previously on Catfish TV' montage to show her being dragged underwater and forced to watch death, or feel her meat melting off her bones.

"You aren't here." Her words were a puff of mist, letters bending and fragmenting the further they got from her lips.

"I'm wherever you are, love."

"It's not real."

"Of course it's real. I'll prove it." And he leaned closer, closer, his pointy nose piercing through the last, misty shreds of her speech. His lips against her forehead like lava while his hands on her face pressed harder. Melting, she was melting in his heat. Her flesh turned viscous and plopped onto her *WTF?!* shoulders. There wasn't any blood, only the thin, pale fluid that seeped around the edges of a wound sometimes.

"We'll always be together, you and me, here beneath the willow tree."

And she could hear the swish of willow leaves brushing the water, the rustle of the cranes in their nest in the upper branches, and things going plop in the water. Maybe this was the reality hidden beneath the stitches and seams. Her bones broke into sharp-edged mineral dust beneath the pressure of his palms. No. She was a puddle of glass beneath an unswept ceiling. Puddles couldn't exist underwater and catfish didn't have ceilings. A spider crawled from its web and came to look at her.

"What the fuck is wrong with you?" the spider asked.

"You know," she replied, because she could see a reflection of herself glittering in each of the spider's eight eyes. "I'm a puddle."

"What you are is crazy." The spider prodded at her with one of its pedipalps.

"I can't help it. They won't leave me alone—Arno and his narrator won't leave me alone."

"We still don't know exactly what happened," Enzo said. "Arno had asked Maggie to use her invisibility to shield him several times before. He was a telepath, and he said her power helped to make everyone else's thoughts less intrusive."

"No, he said it muted the voices completely," Maggie said. "It was a mother's hug for him too."

"Which always seemed weird because Maggie's power is... uncomfortable, at best." Enzo sniffed. "People used to joke about it, say he was crazy to enjoy being in her shield. But something went wrong that night. We heard him screaming first, and a couple of us were already on our way there to see what was happening when Maggie started screaming too."

"I wasn't screaming. I was watching episode one on TV with the catfish."

"When we got to the island... Maggie was on her knees, her skin peeling off her muscles. The look on Arno's face... Puleng was first to realise it was his power, that Arno was attacking us telepathically, giving us hallucinations. He always seemed like a nice guy before that night, not that he spoke much, but he was helpful and reliable. We shot him dead, nothing else we could do, but the damage was done in Maggie's case."

Hadn't Enzo's head floated away? How was he speaking without lungs to send air through his mouth for shaping words with? If a decapitated head revolved through the air with enough speed, could it still speak? And if it could achieve such speed, could it still open its jaw? Maggie didn't speak maths very well but she sensed an impossibility in the marrying of those two questions.

"So he went crazy and now she's crazy too?" Freddy snorted.

"Something like that. We don't know what sent Arno over the edge but his attack did this to Maggie. She developed psychosis, became paranoid. I read everything I could about it but none of the books cover telepathic assault as a cause."

"It's the unreality, isn't it?" Maggie asked the spider, but the spider had returned to its web and was wrapping up some small prey in silk.

"...cut open my face while I was sleeping," Enzo continued,

"and she screamed at Jadine because she thought she'd poisoned her food..."

A sigh brushed over Maggie, warm enough to mist her surface. She didn't like the way it clung to her or the desperate taste of the condensation it caused.

"...tried to make sure someone was always with her but it didn't help. We couldn't help her get better, but we also couldn't let her carry on hurting us."

She swirled around until the pieces of the puddle made sense. Here was a leg and there was a gall bladder. Toes went onto the ends of feet and the hepatic artery connected to the liver.

"...fix this?"

Glue was required, and some swearing and staples, but piece by piece, Maggie became whole once more.

"I don't think you can."

"I just did," Maggie muttered to herself, attaching her right thumb to her palm. "Why are they always watching when you screw up but never when you do something right?"

"What are you talking about?"

"Life." She looked Freddy in the eyes. The intensity of the colour in his pupils had muted to a vivid magenta now. It clashed with his brown irises.

Freddy shook his head and looked past her. "Even if she wanted to help, she's too messed up to do it."

"No. A thousand visions can't all be lies," Rob said. "She's banished the origin of the shadows in all of them, every single one. So she'll do it now that we've found her, we just don't know what choices and events will lead us to that outcome."

Maggie couldn't even see the line where Rob had reattached his head to his neck.

"She's not a bad person—"

"Yes, I am." She frowned at Enzo. Unlike Rob, the silver hinges keeping his head on his neck were marked and obvious.

"No, Maggie." Enzo shook his head. The hinges moved with the motion, wrinkling then slicing through his skin, and finally sliding beneath it. They were no longer visible then.

"...seen for myself how hard you've worked to help others. Everyone you found and brought back to the zoo? You saved their lives. That isn't something that just goes away."

"I've always been a bad person. You didn't know me before."

"I know you now."

"No, you don't, Enzokuhle. You haven't seen me or spoken to me since you kicked me out. Who do you think you know? Maggie that was? She doesn't live here, asshole. I do."

Enzo flinched.

"And I'm done with this."

Invisibility was safety, was a bubble in the noise where she could be free. She pulled that safety tight around her. The men expressed their suffering with the usual array of gross noises but only Enzo stumbled for the kitchen door. She kicked him hard enough to send him sprawling onto the back step.

"Maggie, please." He looked back over his shoulder, one eye pulled down at the outer edge by a tendril of scar tissue. Once, his puppy-dog look would've melted her heart but what heart she had left was immune to such things now.

"Maggie, please search for other survivors, Maggie, please check the old supermarkets for safe food, Maggie, please map out the places where the leopard and buffalo roam." Maggie ground her heel into Enzo's lower back. "It's always 'Maggie, please' until Maggie is the one who needs help."

"I didn't have a choice!" Enzo pressed up on his hands and

clawed at the dirt. "It was a unanimous vote."

"Unanimous? Everyone wanted to exile me?"

"Everyone was afraid of what you might do next. You were hurting people, Maggie."

Maggie stepped aside and let Enzo scramble away from her. Everyone? But she'd stayed up past dawn with Jadine to figure out how to turn dandelion roots into fake coffee, and she'd cried with Faizel when they had to tell him that Charleen died giving birth to Bibi. She'd scoured both Hypers for Crunchie chocolates to cheer Hachi up after her dog died. She'd helped Tina gather everyone together for games of marandas and skipping. She'd hunted feral beef with Luan, and he'd shown her how to shoot a gun. The memories vibrated along the spike through her chest so they had to be real. She'd never have hurt any of them, that was a lie. If they'd all helped to exile her, then their betrayal was real too.

Maggie returned to the house for her spear—a machete secured to a stout pole. Puleng was still missing, confirmation that this was still false. Nothing she did mattered in unreality. Rob and Freddy were gone too, but she heard their heavy footsteps retreating into the house, and further still, to a distance greater than what the house encompassed.

The sound Enzo made when she stabbed her spear through his hand was more of a soprano inhalation than a scream. The stitches were showing again.

"If you were real, I'd tell you that you never needed to be afraid of me until now." She pulled her spear free.

"I'm real. Maggie, I'm real!"

If she killed him now, would he return to haunt her in another false reality, or would he get the message and leave her alone?

"I think you should be a warning," she told him. "You people exiled me out of fear, so I will give you all a reason to be afraid."

She liked the way he whimpered, and the way it flowed into him hastily groping for the car door and locking himself inside. It made her feel powerful. He'd come here to plead for help he didn't deserve and it was fitting that he leave bleeding and frightened. Maggie put one hand to her head, near the back of her skull. Was there a specific place in her mind that he'd return to when this unreality ended? It was a thought filled with comforting implications that she might be able to cut out the madness Arno left her with.

But first, she had to deal with the other two. And fetch the samp and curry Puleng had asked for. Maggie headed back inside.

"Freddy, Rob?" She used a nearly threadbare kitchen towel to wipe away the blood on her spear. "Have you already gone back into my head?"

She waited for an answer, or footsteps. Or roaring and claws hooking on the carpets. When the silence grew bright, staring eyes and a fluffy tail, Maggie decided she'd waited long enough. She took her backpack from the cupboard near the door and set off to do good and dutiful things for Puleng.

Chicken Bones

Maggie returned to the nature reserve near dawn, dragging a bundle packed with supplies. There was an olive-green tent set up in the beam shining from the solar-powered floodlight attached to the wall above her bedroom window. It was both mountain and molehill, highly improbable but so realistic. There were even dirt marks on the fabric.

The light in the kitchen was off. Why would Puleng have turned the light off while it was still dark? Maggie shrugged off the lengths of rope she'd looped around her shoulders to drag the supplies and frowned at the unlit lamp. Maybe the battery died. It shouldn't have died if it was two bars when she turned it on.

Maggie took out the battery pack's solar panel and set it up outside to charge. The tent was still there. She stalked a slow circle around it, searching for flaws in the fabric. There were voices inside it, men's voices, and the rusting, shuffling sounds of movement that suggested there were bodies producing the voices.

"Margaret?"

That voice belonged to the guy... the one with the beard. Maggie looked at her hands. The lines in her palms were all where they were supposed to be. She touched her fingers to the imprints where the ropes had dug into her shoulders while dragging the supplies. It hurt.

The sound of a zipper came from the other side of the tent. She circled around again and stared at the man's head where it protruded through the flap.

"It is you," he said, squirming a little "Would you be so kind as to deactivate your power?"

Rob was his name, or was it Freddy? It was Rob. Freddy was the other one, with the horns.

"Please?" His gaze flickered about, searching, falling on her shadow.

Maggie released her shield and braced against the fear that washed in to replace it. "Why are you still here?"

"Because you can save us."

Maggie stepped back. Was this a continuation of the last episode of unreality, or had it never ended?

"I don't want to save anyone," she said. "In fact, I'm happy to eat popcorn and watch them all die."

"I know, and I'm so sorry for the suffering you've endured to make you feel that way. Enzo told me what happened with the telepath—"

Maggie turned away and ran back inside. Whatever the reason she was seeing this guy again, or still seeing him—why didn't they pursue her last night if it was 'still'?—she wasn't going to talk about Arno. Having his ghost in her head, wrecking the place like a rockstar in a hotel room, was bad enough.

Puleng was sitting at the kitchen table when she entered.

"Did you tell those people they could camp in the front yard?" Maggie asked.

"No. I said they should come inside but they didn't want to because of you."

Maggie cringed at the accusatory tone in Puleng's voice and squatted to untie the ropes holding the supply bundle together. It didn't make sense. She gripped one part of a knot and pulled on it to loosen it. This was what she needed to do in her head, but where had those knots gone off to now?

"And? Aren't you going to say something?"

"I got the samp." She pulled out a sack of samp, only lightly chewed by rats, and set it on the floor.

"Good, that means we'll have plenty of food for our guests. Now, go out there and invite them in."

"But Mme..."

Puleng's eyes rounded and she shook her finger at Maggie. "Don't you argue with me! Must I teach you manners like you're a small child?"

"No," Maggie sighed. "I'm sorry, I..." but she didn't want to admit to Puleng that she hadn't believed they were real. Still wasn't sure they were real, but Puleng could see them.

"What if they're dangerous?"

Puleng snorted. "We're more dangerous, girl, and they'll learn that very fast if they come with nonsense."

Her arguments were all dead so Maggie had to comply. She stomped outside and stopped before the tent once again. The flap was closed now. That detail felt important. It had been open before and now it wasn't. Had it been open before? Had she spoken to Rob just now or had it all happened in her head? She pressed her fingertips against the fabric, felt it slide against her callouses.

"Hey, you in the tent," she said. "It's Freddy and Rob, right?"

"That's correct." The entrance to the tent zipped open and Rob's head poked out. It looked exactly the same as when it poked out before. Maybe poked out before.

"You can... stay. Inside. If you want."

"Are you sure?" Rob frowned.

"I don't like it. We can't trust her." Freddy muttered from somewhere inside. "Remember what Enzo said? She'll kill us in our sleep."

"Look, Puleng wants you to stay in the house so you're welcome there for as long as she says so. I personally don't give a shit so long as she knows I came out here and invited you like she wanted me to."

She walked away before Rob could reply and returned to the kitchen. Puleng looked up at her with arched eyebrows.

"I told them they should stay inside but I can't force them to do it, unless you want me to?"

Puleng tutted. "You were rude to them, weren't you?"

"Of course not." She bent to unpack the tins of food she'd brought home.

"And now you're lying to me."

"I am not!"

"Margaret?"

Rob was standing in the doorway behind her.

"Come in." She gestured for him to enter and shuffled to one side to continue unpacking.

"I..." Rob cleared his throat, said nothing, sighed.

Maggie placed more tins on the counter, what remained of their labels turned to face Puleng. "See? Plenty of curry too. Even the hot one you like so much."

"Excuse me?"

She side-eyed Rob over her shoulder. "I wasn't talking to you."

"I see." His face sagged as he surveyed the kitchen. "Right. Margaret, I think I should be completely honest with you. I was not expecting to find you in such... peculiar circumstances. And I don't know what to do now, considering your current situation, and although it's clear you don't want to be involved in destroying the shadows, I can't just give up on you, or leave you to carry on living in this... state, not when—"

"This state?" She stood and faced him. "I thought you were going to be honest; instead you're using manners to lie. You mean that I'm crazy, so just say it."

Rob ran a hand over his beard. "Crazy is a nasty, unspecific term. It was demeaning and ignorant in the world before the Change and it's demeaning and ignorant now."

"Debating the meaning of words and how kind they are doesn't change the fact that you're scared of what I'll do to you." She moved closer to him. "And you should be scared. Your friend was wrong about me killing you in your sleep but only because I'd make you run first."

"Maggie!"

She flinched at the anger in Puleng's voice.

"You are so rude!" Puleng shuffled towards her.

"But you heard how he spoke to me."

"With kindness and care, yes. This person wants to help you."

Maggie sucked her teeth. "If he wants to help me then it's only because doing that helps himself."

"That's not true, Margaret."

Maggie started to roll her eyes at Rob, but stopped so Puleng wouldn't have another reason to shout at her.

"Yes, this world needs your help, and yes, your victory over the origin of shadows will ultimately serve me, but I didn't know you were hurt and now..."

He'd been flapping his hands about while he spoke but now they froze, awkward birds in flight, slowly folding together into a prayer.

"...now I wonder if maybe a part of the reason I was led to find you is because there's something I can do to help you heal," he finished.

Maggie looked at his face, so earnest and open. "You are full of... nonsense."

"I understand your reluctance to believe me, but I do want to help." He pressed a hand to his chest. "I volunteered with an outreach program for troubled youth before the Change, so I may know some coping techniques that can help you."

Maggie laughed. Coping techniques? Was that the name of a magical stick she could hit everything with to test whether it was real? Was this why Rob and Freddy were here? Their presence her brain's way of trying to help her?

No. They were real... she'd forgotten. Puleng saw them so they had to be real. His hands were real hands and where that one pressed against his chest he'd feel warmth, pressure. If the contact were transferred, if he touched her, then she'd feel those things too. Would he feel the fear itching just beneath the top layers of her skin? Could he see it spreading up from her wrists?

"Life can get better for you, Margaret."

There was sincerity in his voice, and conviction. This was... something... something abstract but almost tangible. It was a bud of hope somewhere just below her stomach, a warmth, a concept that slipped away down a water slide before she could catch it in a box. The catfish didn't come to eat it, and that was strange.

"Margaret?"

His hand was warm. It worsened the itching of her fear and awoke an instinctive desire to bite him, but she didn't. Instead, she turned to Puleng. Puleng would know what to do, what to say, what to be, but Puleng wasn't there.

"Mme?" She hadn't heard or seen her leave. Why would she leave when Maggie needed her? She crossed the kitchen to stare down the passage but Puleng wasn't shuffling across the thin carpet and the light in her bedroom was off.

"Mme, o kae?" She knocked on the door to Puleng's bedroom then opened it.

Empty. Empty of Puleng's bed, her clothes, the huge dressing table with its window-sized mirror and the cosmetics that lined it. There were footsteps imprinted in the dust on the floor. She couldn't breathe right: the air was too quick. Some of it leaked into her head where the pressure of it built in the space between the membrane surrounding her brain and the fused bones of her skull. Would those same bones become shrapnel if her head exploded, and would she be able to piece it back together afterwards?

No. She was freaking out for nothing. Puleng was just outside. She had to be.

"Puleng?" she shouted as she jogged back down the passage and into the kitchen.

"Margaret, who are you looking for?" Rob asked as she strode past him. "The only people here are you, me and Freddy."

The pressure in her head was painful now. Puleng wasn't walking down the path leading to the vegetable patch. She wouldn't be; at this time of the evening she'd be feeding the chickens. Maggie jogged to the corner of the house and around it, to the chicken hok. Puleng wasn't there either and all the chickens were gone, no, dead. Their small bones lay in disorder across the floor of the cage. Tall weeds grew in the dirt and a spider's web glittered in the first rays of dawn.

"Margaret! The sun!"

Rob's shout was distant and every bit as nonsensical as the state of the chicken hok. Puleng always told her when a chicken died. How could this have happened? Was it because she didn't dig out the grubs for them yet? No, only weeks of neglect could cause this, but hadn't she struggled to sleep last week because the chickens had been clucking and squabbling outside her window?

It couldn't be real. She opened the door to the chicken hok and reached inside, wrapping her fingers around a thin, bleached bone. A wishbone. It reminded her of family dinners when she was small; creepy uncle Elijah giving her and her cousin, Nadia, the wishbone to break between them and the fucked-up smile he gave Nadia if she got the bigger piece.

Rob screamed her name. Maggie looked up and saw a shadow approaching her, wobbly as a newborn calf in the early morning light. Spiralling kudu horns as long as sapling trees crowned its wedge-shaped head. It pressed against the tall fence surrounding the yard. Bulges of inky shadow formed between the metal slats then oozed over them when the creature began pushing through. One leg split below the knee when the shadow pushed it through the fence, reforming into two lower legs with two clawed paws. When the shadow was halfway through the fence, it rose up the slats like a carousel horse and landed soundlessly in the tall weeds.

There was a drunken grace in the way the shadow stumbled toward her. Legs crisscrossed and intersected as it picked up speed. The split in the one foreleg travelled higher, creating a third front leg that migrated to the centre of the creature's chest. Its lower jaw dropped open like a suddenly loosened trapdoor, revealing a large proboscis-like tongue. It lunged at her and froze in midair.

"Get off your gat and get inside."

Freddy spared her an angry glance when he spoke. He was using her spear to pin the shadow. Sunlight reflected off the machete blade where it had pierced through to the creature's other side. He looked at her... her shield wasn't up. And if this was real... it couldn't be real.

Freddy kicked the shadow. Fine shards of grey burst out from the impact and tickled across her arm. Pinning a shadow was only half the job; once caught in place, it had to be shattered. Puleng, who had been throwing pebbles at noisy doves when the Apocalypse hit and gained the power of never missing a shot because of it, had been excellent at pinning. Was excellent. No, it was had been... had been excellent ranged back-up in general, until Arno attacked. Maggie had watched him make Puleng stab herself on a giant flatscreen TV; it had been a cautionary advert break during episode twenty or twenty-one. One of the catfish in Loch Logan had spat the TV out in front of her while she was drowning and that was both real and true: Puleng had died with her own knitting needles pushed through her throat. There had been bubbles and whistling—the tune from some old movie about a bridge. There'd been an unforgettable shlucking sound when she pulled one of the needles out, and a clarity of hopelessness in Puleng's eyes.

Maggie grabbed a loose brick lying outside the chicken hok and bashed it against the shadow's head. Its upper jaw shattered.

"Just get inside!"

But it was almost impossible to pin a monster this size and shatter it alone. If Maggie left him, the shadow would turn on him the moment he released it. Freddy would be sucked up like soup and leaving him to die like that felt wrong somehow. Puleng would've expected more from Maggie, she'd expect her to do *that*.

Maggie rolled to her feet and circled round to put a hand on Freddy's shoulder.

"Brace yourself," she said, and gave him exactly one breath to do it in before shrugging her shield on. Freddy disappeared when she did.

He shivered beneath her hand. "What are you doing to me?"

"My shield is covering both of us. Come on."

He actually growled when he tugged the spear free. "This better not make me crazy like that Arno guy."

"He hid in my shield plenty of times before he lost his shit and it never hurt him. Don't blame my power for his madness."

The shadow stumbled away, its shattered jaw already reforming. Maggie fought the impulse to release Freddy from her shield before he could try to hurt her, but he just turned, revolving around her. Maggie moved with him, aware of his presence only through the way she felt his arm move beneath her hand.

"Freddy, Margaret?" Rob still stood at the back door, holding it open just wide enough to peer outside.

"We're coming," Freddy snapped.

"Step back from the door," Maggie added.

Rob retreated. She and Freddy bumped into each other when they both reached for the door.

"Go," Maggie said, releasing him from the protection of her shield when she pushed him toward the door.

He ducked inside and she followed, leaning back against the door to shut it.

"What is wrong with you?" Freddy shouted. He'd shed his horns. Maybe they were deer horns and not antelope, as she'd assumed.

"A lot." Maggie dropped her shield and moved toward him with her hand out. "My spear."

Freddy's lips pulled back into a snarl and he twisted the spear so she could grasp the blunt end.

"Freddy," Rob said, a warning in his tone.

"Fuck that." Freddy pointed at her. "You are fucking mad, just like all the crazies that lost their head when they got powers."

"No, it happened to me a long time after and only because Arno attacked me. Maybe his power made him crazy, but he never told me how he got his power. He was probably a creepy stalker type, all things considered, so the crazy might've come first." Maggie closed her hands around the shaft of her spear hard enough to feel the pull of muscles and tendon in her fingers.

"When it happened doesn't matter."

This spear was real. She lowered it and was about to slide the blade across the back of her wrist when a hand reached out to grab it.

"Don't," Rob said. "You're going to hurt yourself."

"I want to see if I bleed," she replied. "I should see if you bleed too."

"Is that a threat?" Freddy stepped forward.

"No, it isn't." Rob waved Freddy off without looking away from her. "You want to know if we're real, correct?"

"I need to know if I'm real first."

"That's sensible." Rob nodded. "How can I help you with that?"

Her head hurt too much to think but thoughts cartwheeled through her brain all the same. She scanned the kitchen. Puleng wasn't here. Maybe she'd never been here, not even once, because she was cloth wrapped sticks in the ground and a flock of red weaver birds. Not a single breath Maggie took gave her the amount of air she needed. She sat at the table and spread her hands across the surface. How long had it been? Almost a year, maybe, because she remembered struggling to start the vegetable garden in the cooling days of early autumn. They'd eaten pigeons often because the birds were morons and Puleng never missed... no. Puleng wasn't here. Puleng was never here but Maggie remembered retrieving pigeons Mme had killed. How could she remember something that didn't happen? Did it work the same way as when something happened that you didn't remember?

"Margaret."

Rob was sitting across from her now, his hand held out with the palm facing up. She leaned in to study lifelines and heartlines. Rob's callouses were a map of things done repetitively, actions taken which then imprinted in the clay of reality. She took his hand in hers and turned it over to locate the scars where reality had imprinted on him in return. There were thin white lines and a jagged, star-shaped pucker of scar tissue near the base of his thumb that reminded her of a cigarette burn.

"Our world is strange and filled with monsters, and it's natural to doubt the reality of all this," Rob said. "It's natural to question the sanity of what I've asked you to do and I'm sorry I wasn't more considerate in my approach. I didn't know you were wounded. My visions never showed me that."

"You still would've come looking for me?" Maggie asked.

"Of course."

He seemed surprised that she would ask. Maggie glanced sideways to where Puleng usually sat. Habit. The empty chair offered no guidance, but she knew what Puleng would've expected from her. She vaguely recognised the balloon of feeling in her chest and what it meant. Balloons came with ribbons because feeling cared for was something you had to hold onto.

She drew back her hand and stood.

"You can sleep in the lounge," she said, moving across the kitchen to show them the way. "There's enough food. The toilet works, kind of. It uses a drain dug out back but I haven't fetched more water from the river for flushing yet."

"What are the chances you'll kill us in our sleep?" Freddy scowled at her as she drew level with him.

Maggie shrugged. "You can always make a run for your tent."

"Monsters outside or the lunatic inside. Great options," he muttered.

Before and After

The threadbare Batman printed on Maggie's comforter sat up to watch her while she slept.

"You need to clean your room," Batman said.

Maggie shook her head.

"Eish, Maggie. You have to clean your room!" Batman's voice boomed as he grew taller, his weight pressing down on her chest. "We can't have guests when your room looks like this."

"Who's coming to visit?"

Batman leaned in close enough to smell the garlic on his breath. "They are coming. So you have to make scones, and tea, and tidy up the whole house before 9 o'clock."

She'd never have enough time. Maggie tried to sit but Batman was too heavy. So heavy she couldn't get enough breath to ask him to move.

"Hurry up, Maggie. Time is moving without you."

And she could hear it now, a tick, tick, ticking growing louder, closer. She kicked and bucked to get Batman off her chest, but he was stoically immobile despite his insistence that she hurry. Time chattered its teeth, eating towards her through the wall behind her head. The rhythmic crunch of bricks and fizzle of electric cables filled the room.

Batman's shoulders bowed and he hugged himself. "It's too loud in here," he whispered, but that wasn't Batman's voice any more. "Help me, Maggie, it's too loud."

She walked to where Arno hunched near the edge of the water. She watched herself put a hand on his shoulder and raise her shield around them both. She tried to run—she knew what came next—but she couldn't even turn away.

His hand slid around her waist, gripping and groping. He was way too close. When she pushed him away...Arno threw back his head and screamed. His eyes bulged out of their sockets, supported by raw nerve bundles. They wrapped up her arm and Maggie was also screaming now. She watched the flesh melt away from her other self wherever the nerve bundles touched, saw Arno's eyeballs split open to reveal rows of needle-sharp teeth that sank into her other self's throat. The catfish crawled up the riverbank to take her away.

Maggie leapt from her bed. She ran for the door but the handle slapped her to the floor. The windows were sealed to keep the light out. She was trapped.

"Wat maak jy?"

Freddy stared down at her from the doorway. The thorns lining the doorframe sprouted vines that spread across the walls, obscuring the peeling white paint. Dark green leaves and stargazer lily flowers unfurled from the vines as they spread.

Lilies didn't grow on vines. She braved the thorns to grab Freddy's wrist and set her fingers against his pulse. His heart beat steadily beneath her fingertips.

"It wasn't a zombie apocalypse, you know."

Maggie peered at the closest flower. Its anthers were glass. Tiny LED lights flashed out a pattern at the tips. "Do you know Morse code?"

"Who the fuck does?"

"Enzo. He knows everything he reads forever; that's his power."

"He must've been a huge nerd before the Change."

"He was studying for an exam when it happened."

"What were you doing?"

"Me? I was stealing my mom's car but the mascara lady was there... no, you're real." She turned back to Freddy. "That's the wrong story if you're real."

Freddy arched an eyebrow. "Oh, you have different stories for what happened? Which one's the truth?"

"I'm not sure." Surely the woman's eyelashes didn't flap like moth wings. Her stilettos couldn't have been sharp enough to gouge holes in the cement. The tick tock dog couldn't have screamed like that when Maggie hit it with her mom's car. Nothing could scream like that.

His lips pursed and he gave her an assessing look. "Because some telepath messed with your head?"

She whirled away from him. "Why are you here? I thought you were scared of me."

"Wary, not scared. You were making a lawaai so I came to see what was happening. Did you have a nightmare?"

She didn't know how to answer him. Was that really just a nightmare? She'd gone to bed after showing Freddy and Rob the lounge, and she was wearing the sports bra she usually slept in so maybe it was just a bad dream. She looked back at Freddy. He was waiting for her answer but Puleng would... would have killed her for standing in front of a man she barely knew in only her underwear. Stupid things like that mattered to people when you weren't invisible.

"Maybe." Maggie picked through the clothes on her chair and pulled on a pair of shorts.

"That answers one of my questions, anyway."

She grabbed a tank top from the pile and sniffed it. "How many questions do you have?"

"Only one more. Do you want revenge on the people at the zoo?"

Maggie pulled the shirt over her head. Revenge? Wasn't it called justice when you were the victim?

"You do, don't you?" Freddy's voice was closer, lower: more secretive. "Will you kill the shadows if I help you with that?"

His horns had grown back overnight, a dark brown striped with cream that shone like they'd been polished. Somebody who looked so demonic shouldn't radiate such sincerity.

"You must have thought about it," he continued, "daydreamed about what you'd like to do to them."

Maggie shook her head. "Not really, not like you mean. I just want my home back."

"You mean the zoo?"

"I was the first one there. Me and Sam. He's dead now, so it belongs to me."

"If I help you take it back, will you kill the shadows?"

He was temptation offering a misdirection of options. She watched the lights in the lilies flashing like satellites. Sometimes she still saw lights moving in the sky, crossing the stars, racing for distant horizons. Were they real? Was this real? She reached out to touch one of the thorns but froze with her finger poised above the sharp point. She couldn't do this anymore. She couldn't question the validity of every moment she lived.

"I'm still waiting for an answer."

Freddy smiled at her but this was a lie, an empty gesture. The falseness of it rippled across his eyes and curdled the earnestness she'd seen in him before. It was a sad change.

"I don't have any answers." Maggie moved past him into the passage. The vines followed her along the walls until she reached the kitchen. Rob was there, opening tins and throwing their contents into a pot.

"Good evening, Margaret," he said. "Are you well?"

"Just 'Maggie' is fine." She circled around to look at the torn labels on the tins. Tinned samp and beans, tinned vegetables and tinned chicken curry. "Tell me what happened in your vision, when you saw me."

Rob frowned a little. "Are you sure you want to hear this?"

"I asked, didn't I?"

He nodded and carried the pot towards the back door. The sky was pale as a washed-out sheet and the setting sun was an amber traffic light hidden by the hills. The fire flickered within the ring of bricks she'd built near the back step to contain it and licked along the bottom of the pot as soon as Rob set it down.

"You're always outside, in the midday sun," Rob said. "The exact place varies, but the original shadow always appears before you—"

"What is the original shadow?"

"Well, the Change was not as random as it seemed." Rob reached across to stir the pot. "There is a singular power behind it, an entity not unlike the shadow creatures, but more powerful, more substantial, I believe."

"Like some kind of shadow king?" She crouched down nearby.

"Exactly. The original shadow. From what I've seen in my visions, it's a creature not from this dimension."

"Then what is it?"

"I don't know, not exactly. I can't see those details well

enough to understand what the origin of the shadows is or why it caused the Change." Rob frowned at the pot. "I think it's something akin to a god, or a demon. Something supernatural."

"And I supposedly can destroy this fairy tale monster?"

"No. It cannot be destroyed, as far as I know, but you can banish it back to the place it comes from."

"But why? What's my motivation? I don't get why this would be the story I make up for myself."

"This is still real, Maggie." Rob turned to look at her. The light from the fire swirled across his face like ribbons. The white hairs in his beard were actually worms. Maggie could see them wriggling.

"Right. I forgot." One of the worms was investigating the lower edge of Rob's lip. "Isn't that ticklish?"

They stared at each other in silence for what felt like a long time before Rob cleared his throat.

"I don't know your reasons for facing the origin shadow. I always assumed you would be willing to save the few of us that still survive."

"This shitty dorp isn't the whole world," Freddy said.

He was watching her from the doorway to the kitchen. Horns had sprouted from his elbows too now. Maybe horn growing was his power.

"It's my whole world," Maggie replied. "I've never been anywhere else."

"And that's your excuse for being small-minded?"

"Freddy..."

Freddy looked at Rob and pulled a face. "This is real talk. We can't go back to life before the Change but we can make survival easier. Or she can, if she can get over herself."

Rob sighed and put a hand to his face.

"Seriously," Freddy looked at her with narrowed eyes. "If you hate the people here so much that you'll let everyone else suffer just to spite them, then just get back at them and be done with it."

"You should know better than to advocate for vengeance, Freddy," Rob said.

"I'm advocating for whatever convinces her to kill the shadows," Freddy replied.

He was afraid. The thought hit her like the minibus taxi that had crashed into her mom's car when the Apocalypse killed everyone. But he'd still come to pin the shadow when it was about to eat her, when she'd forgotten her shield was furled inside her belly. Shadows ate people; that was true even though it was something she usually didn't need to worry about. She'd seen it close up when the rabbit shadow with the hadeda ibis head leapt from the reeds near the water and latched onto Sam's face. Her hands had slipped through its body. Her hands remembered how cold it was inside, and gritty as kinetic sand. By the time she remembered to pin it, by the time she'd drawn Sam's knife from his belt, Sam was a deflated skin balloon. He also slipped through her hands and slid into the water where the catfish waited.

Catfish ate everything, except her.

"What does it look like?" Maggie asked. "The original shadow."

Rob had his mouth open and a finger pointed at Freddy, but he turned to look at her now. The worms in his beard stopped their writhing to watch her too.

"It looks like a person."

"Why would a god, demon creature look like a person?"

"I don't know. I don't have all the answers, Maggie. All I know is what I've seen, and what I've been able to interpret from those visions."

"Okay, so I use my shield to banish it?"

Rob nodded. "All the shadows die then. They turn into dust as though they've been shattered."

"And it goes back to... where, exactly? Australia?"

"No. I don't know where it comes from, but I think it's from a different dimension."

"So, the USA?"

Freddy snorted but Rob put a hand to his forehead and sighed.

"That's where all the freaky shit happens in movies. It's logical that this origin comes from something weird over there."

"Your questions are valid, Maggie, and I wish I could give you equally valid answers but I simply don't know where the origin comes from, or what it is. I'm trying to make educated guesses based on what I've seen and information I've gathered from esoteric books along the way, but it's still just guesswork." He poked the spoon around in the pot. "All I know for certain is that the origin is a creature with immense power, that it used that power to create the Change, and that you can destroy the shadows it brought to life by banishing the origin with your power."

"And you think that will make the world a better place?"

"It will make the world a safer place. People could go outside in the daylight again. We'll be able to rebuild our societies, restart the economy."

Economy, that greedy altar bosses sacrificed their staff on. He said it like this was something she should want. Society was the name of the knife Enzo stabbed into her back. Before that, it was the mascara lady's griping.

Before, what she remembered most about before was loneliness, a mother that cried about bills and came home from night shifts too tired to notice Maggie had been partying all night, anger, and a hunger for something good. It was shit in a way that didn't compare to the shit of survival now, where there were still shining stars of happiness in her memories of that other before, before Arno. She wanted to tell Rob these things, but the train carrying the words from her brain to her tongue broke down somewhere behind her right ear.

"...trading with each other, sharing our unique abilities to help each other build and grow," Rob was saying now. "Eventually we could travel to other countries too, rediscover a sense of global community."

This man was unhinged. "Have you actually seen that future?"

"I have, and worse futures too, but those were before I started seeing you."

She looked over at Freddy. His expression was unreadable but she understood that he would do whatever it took to convince her to help them. His motives were linear, easier to follow than Rob's skewed sense of human nature. However, Rob's optimism and drive to help would be like cement if she let it, ensuring she'd always have a place with these people, that she'd never be lonely again. These people could be her new people, but only if she figured out how to hold onto them after she killed their shadow man.

Maggie stood and stretched. "I have fake coffee. It's made from dandelions. Do you want some?"

"That would be nice," Rob said.

Freddy nodded. He stepped aside to let her pass and followed her inside.

"I meant what I said," he muttered, "I'll help you take back your home, or whatever you need to do, if you'll help us."

Maggie reached around the fist-sized ball of woodlice in the cupboard and grabbed the dandelion coffee tin. "I don't want to hurt anyone."

Freddy cackled. "Ja, you stabbed Enzo right through his hand because you don't want to hurt people."

What a strange thing to say. And why say it at all when she knew it wasn't true? Who was he lying for?

"How do you people even know Enzo?"

"Rob's visions led us to your people."

"They're not my people anymore."

"Ja, ja," he leaned back against the counter and crossed his arms, "but you don't want to hurt them, apparently. What do you want then?"

Maggie opened the lid of the dandelion coffee tin. A gigantic, dried-blood red cockroach head peered up at her from the bottom.

"After a century of waiting, I am finally free," the cockroach head said.

"It can't have been longer than a week," Maggie replied. "What did you do with the coffee?"

"You're holding it in your hands," Freddy said. "And what about a week?"

"It has been a century since I was imprisoned," the cockroach head replied. "Look."

It used its antennae to point at the sides of the tin, where Maggie now noticed tally marks carved into the metal.

"But now I am free once more, free to seek out those who imprisoned me and exact my—"

Maggie shut the lid and passed the tin to Freddy. "It's your problem now."

"In what world is coffee a problem? Even fake coffee."

"I'm not talking about the coffee." She leaned back against the counter and watched a pattern of small bulges appear on the wall opposite her. "You asked me what I want, didn't you?"

"I did."

"I don't know." The base of each bulge blushed red. "I want to be okay, and safe, and not lonely. I want to know what's real and what isn't."

"How can it be so difficult to tell the difference?"

Maggie shrugged. Fine lines criss-crossed the planes between the reddened bulges. It was a pattern she felt intimately familiar with, although she couldn't say why.

"But surely things that are real make sense, and things that aren't don't."

"Exactly." A black cap formed at the peak of each bulge and Maggie suddenly understood. They were pimples.

"If you're agreeing with me then what's the problem?"

"You need to find the seams before you can pick at the stitches." She began to pace, eyeing the pimples. "And you need to catch the ideas in boxes before they go down the water slides."

"What?"

"The catfish eat everything."

"It's like we're not even talking the same language."

"It doesn't matter because I can still understand." One of the pimples started throbbing. She hooked her fingers around his elbow and pushed him towards the door.

"I need mugs," he said.

"None of that will matter if those pimples erupt."

"If the whats do what now?" He dug his heels in and turned, leaning in to look at her.

"The pimples," she repeated. "That one's throbbing."

He put one hand to his face. "You're having one of your episodes right now, aren't you?"

"Am I?" She looked back to the wall. Watery fluid was leaking around the edges of the black cap on the throbbing pimple, but it wasn't throbbing, it was really the skin moving like a chest, raising and falling, breathing.

"I think so."

Maggie placed her hand against the wall. It was cool, pulsing faintly. What sort of creature had skin like this? Humans did. What about hairless cats, or naked molerats? If those creatures had skin like this, did they get pimples?

Freddy's face appeared in front of her. "What do you see?"

"Something with large skin."

"And pimples?"

Maggie nodded.

"Sounds weird."

She looked at the confusion in his eyes, at the skin beneath her palm, and then back at him. She took his hand and pressed it against the skin, right where her own had been a few moments ago. He blinked a few times, lips moving but not saying anything, letting his eyes convey an entire book full of questions instead.

He'd lied about her stabbing Enzo's hand so maybe he was lying about this too, trying to gaslight her into thinking what was real wasn't, but why? Did he think he could use the unreality against her, make her doubt herself even more than what she already did? What could he possibly gain from that?

Or, the skin really wasn't there. Hadn't she decided to stop doing this to herself? If she was going to try to keep these people then maybe she should trust them. But there was a streak of blood in the pimple fluid now, and the cap was arcing outwards.

"Jesus." Maggie fled through the back door, no longer concerned with whether this was unreality or not, or Freddy's safety.

Outside, sparks from the fire drifted on the air of a monochrome world. They whispered to each other as they spiralled together in private dances that carried them up and out of sight.

"Maggie?"

She could dance like that. She didn't even need a partner, just an appropriately sized launcher. Something like that flying fairy toy she had when she was small. Maggie stretched out her arms and there were wings between her fingers now. Maybe they'd always been there, waiting for her to discover them. Birds could fly because their bones were hollow, but Maggie would fly because her skin was a plastic shell surrounding foetid air. She began to float without even pulling the string on her launcher. The sparks from the fire welcomed her into their dance, revolving around her, nestling into her hair. Trails of smoke spiralled around her now, growing thicker as she began to burn. It wasn't even hot but the smell... rotten, rotting, mould on the inside, why would she ever have expected her cooking flesh to smell appetising?

The sparks were swearing at her now. Their vulgar words leaving a brown ooze in the cooking smoke tornado around her.

"How did you survive this long on your own?" Rob asked.

"I had Puleng."

"The woman you were looking for the other day?"

"Eya."

"Will you tell me about her?"

"She's... she's dead."

"That would explain why I never saw her."

Dead. It was shrapnel squirming in her chest and the way the air burned her throat with every breath she took. Puleng had been her rock and her compass since she lost herself to the catfish but she'd never been here so who had been guiding Maggie? Who did Maggie need to mourn?

"I don't know which is the right way anymore."

"Maybe I can help you figure it out."

Maggie looked down the centre of the smoke tornado. Rob squatted at the bottom, his body fused into the fire. Maggie changed the direction of her rotation so she was descending now and landed beside him. Flames danced beneath his skin as though it were just a curtain, a window to a place inside him where everything burned.

"Can you clean me?" she asked. "Like when you put a needle into fire before you use it on a wound?"

"You aren't a needle, Maggie."

She had the urge to dig her nails into his face and part those curtains so she might climb into the flames and be reborn. Or cremated. Either one would work.

"I think I'd like to be a needle." She reached out and traced the dancing flames across his cheek. "One belonging to a seamstress, not a surgeon."

"You want to be used to create something instead of to fix what's hurt?"

"What's hurt can't be fixed." The truth hammered at the centre of her forehead once she'd stated it. "Nothing can be fixed."

The heat from the fire beneath Rob's skin diminished, giving way to a cold certainty that settled across her shoulders. She could never be who she was in either before. Both those Maggies were people from TV with normal, TV lives. The world would never be better either because the shadows were nothing but an inconvenience while the true evil was, and always would be, other people.

"I don't think that's true. The world before the Change was a hard and ugly place, but we have a chance to start over now."

Rob's fire might've gone cold but his eyes burned so brightly that it distracted Maggie from truth's heartbeat, which was still hammering at her forehead.

"The world can be better than it was before. All of us have suffered and seen suffering that's changed who we are. I saw it countless times in the people we met on the way here. Pain can be a catalyst for the darkest parts of someone's personality but most people become more compassionate, more attuned to the hurts of others and, therefore, kinder."

It made sense now. Rob had a star in his head and its light was escaping through his eyes. It penetrated the gaps between the stitches and drove the catfish into hiding. The light made sunsets in her brain that calmed her thoughts to a soothing mauve.

Catfish TV

Maggie walked down the centre of a tarred road. Her palms were sweaty and sticky from holding hands with her people but she dared not loosen her grip. Shadow hyenas with porcupine spines stalked among the rusted cars and they were darn near solid at this time of day.

Maggie walked down the centre of a tarred road. Mom once told her the municipality rebuilt this road when they widened it, which would explain why it was lasting so well. Her palms were sweaty from holding hands with her people for so long. How long had it been?

Maggie walked down the centre of a tarred road. Freddy complained about the heat and the glare from the sun but, when she turned to look at him, he wasn't there.

Maggie walked down the centre of a tarred road, but this time she knew she'd done it before. She led Freddy and Rob into the underground parking area of Mimosa Mall and kicked open the door to the parking management office near the entrance. It was dark inside, and cool, and smelled musty in the way of old paper and dust rather than picked off bones. Maggie released her shield and sat in a corner with her back to the wall. Ribs and intercostal muscles flexed when she breathed. Her heart beat, and she felt her shirt pull when she wiped her palms dry on it.

"Are we close now?" Freddy spoke in the dark nearby, his shoes scuffing on the floor.

"I recognise this building from when Enzo drove us out to meet Maggie," Rob replied.

Something happened before this. Maggie could feel it flapping on the outskirts of 'now', a gauzy, abandoned spiderweb of meaning and context.

"So, we're going to take a break here and carry on to the zoo later?" Freddy asked.

They were going to the zoo?

"Maggie?" Rob said.

"Sure," she replied. "It's hot and my hands feel icky."

Freddy snorted. "Ja, ne. It's weird being outside during the day."

Why were they travelling by day, in her shield?

"But it's also cool being able to walk past all those shadows." Freddy sat down beside her.

"I guess so."

"Are you still good?"

Good. She had too many dark corners to be good. Thorns and pus directed her morals, but no, he hadn't meant good in that context. Every word had a thousand synonyms. Every synonym conveyed a slightly altered meaning. Good was okay, okay was fine, fine was all right. She'd found the right track.

Why had he said 'still', as though there was a time before this when she was okay? She hadn't been okay in years, since way before she met him or Rob.

A hand on her shoulder; too dim to see the owner in this dark room but she could eliminate most tentacle creatures and ghosts, and that left Freddy.

"I don't want to go to the zoo," she told him.

"We just need to see Nico so he can take a look at you," Rob replied from across the room. "That's our priority at this point."

"Nico?"

"Our friend. The healer, remember?"

"Healer? Like a doctor from before?"

"It's his power." Freddy's hand slipped away. "Are you not lekker again?"

"Freddy." Rob's voice carried a warning.

"I'm... a little lost," Maggie replied. "We're going to the zoo. To see your friend because he got a healing power from the Apocalypse?"

Freddy sighed deeply. "You're not a little lost, you're completely off the map."

"That's not what's happening?"

"It is." Rob cleared his throat. "There's no guarantee Nico can help you. I've seen him mend some terrible wounds, and he worked on a woman from the Colesburg community who had kidney stones, but the brain is a complex organ."

"But he might be able to help me?" The hinges on her ribs felt loose and a strange sense of fullness spread through her chest. She'd almost forgotten she had a balloon inside her now and how nice it felt.

"That's what we hope, and why you insisted we come here immediately even though it meant travelling through the middle of the fucking day."

Freddy was a bulgy lump of black in the grey of the room, features indistinct. It didn't sound like her to volunteer to shield them through the daylight, but they were dangling an opportunity to be well again.

"And it was a good idea. Maggie kept us perfectly safe," Rob said.

"What happens next? After Nico tries his power on me, what then?"

Freddy groaned. He shifted beside her, bumping her shoulder, and muttered something about being Pete and repeat stuck on a boat. It was a joke, something an uncle told her when she was small.

Rob cleared his throat. "We've yet to reach an agreement on that."

"Bloemfontein is not a place where you stay; it's a two horse dump you pass through on the way to somewhere better," Freddy said. "And Joburg is a solid lead. It's the first place you've recognised in your visions."

"The future finds you no matter where you are, Freddy. Chasing down destiny doesn't necessarily mean we'll reach it any sooner."

"Kak, man. We came all the way here to chase her down, how is this different?"

"We needed to find Maggie so she could be forewarned about the origin of shadows. We've done that now so the rest is a waiting game."

"I don't want to wait," Freddy said.

"We need to do whatever is best for Maggie."

"Which is why leaving is better. There's nothing here for you, Maggie, except kak memories and people who threw you out like a used tissue."

Would the balloon pop if it got too full, and what would happen to the feelings keeping it inflated if it burst? Perhaps those feelings would fill the rest of her body then, from the tip of her longest toe to the end of the longest hair on her head.

She'd only find out so long as she remained necessary to them.

"There's stuff," she said. "Supplies I've hidden away. Enough to last three people a very long time."

"What?" Rob sounded shocked.

"I've got supplies I've hidden away. It made sense to move it from the shops to places where its more secure and easier to access."

"So you want to stay here so you can be a fly on this city's carcass?" Freddy made a sound of disgust. "Why would you choose to pick at leftovers when you have a choice to do something more, something better?"

Freddy had a point about staying here... and they were offering her a chance to leave with them. Not being alone was far more important than the fear of being in unknown spaces, but Joburg was far away, and why there? She looked into the darkness where she heard Rob shifting, crackling plastic and drinking. There were reasons for going to Joburg specifically. The recognition Freddy mentioned was part of it. There was urgency; it whispered at her words she thought she remembered about racing dawn down the potholed remnants of the highway, and a vision. Rob had another vision of her. She'd faced the shadow king man creature in Joburg this time, or would face him there. Which meant she'd also have to face the afterwards and its problem of how to keep her new people sooner than she'd thought,

"I'm going to pee." Maggie stood and shuffled across to where she thought the door was.

A circle of light appeared before her, roaming across the blinds in the window before settling on the door handle. She could've ventured deeper into the parking area and squatted beside a dead car but Maggie went back out into the light, where the tarnished and broken windows of the Absa building across the road stared down at her. The Bloemspruit river ran beside the building for a few metres before disappearing under the road. It was choked with weeds, invisible as she was, and Maggie was struck by the strangeness of the decision to settle an entire town, which would one day become a city, which would one day become a carcass, because of one trickling stream and some flowers. She looked to where she knew Naval Hill stood, obscured by buildings from this angle, and wondered if the ghosts of British soldiers still lurked there, and what ghosts might've haunted them when this land was taken from people the history books neglected to mention.

People made tiny universes out of the places where they lived. Lives became closed circuits of localised lore and the opinions of communities made up of mascara ladies and Enzos. Even before she'd felt like a stone in the bottom of a tightly laced boot. She'd thought home was the place where you knew every shortcut and the name the neighbours screamed at their dog when it was barking at 2 am. Then she thought home was the place where you made survival more comfortable, the place where you made a family of strangers. Maybe she'd been wrong both times. Maybe home was a place she hadn't found yet.

Maggie looked toward the tall block of flats near the zoo, pissed on Bloemfontein and returned to the parking lot.

They ate and napped, and left when the sun had vanished beyond the horizon but the sky was still blue and mauve. The walk to the zoo wasn't long enough for Maggie's hands to get sweaty from holding onto Freddy and Rob. Fear made her sweat instead. It started with the familiarity of the tall, tall Eucalyptus trees growing around the zoo and Loch Logan, an itch of nervousness that tunnelled through the mould beneath her skin. Her vision zoomed ahead, doing barrel rolls through reeds until she saw the willow tree on the island. The itch became cold wires drawing taut.

"Maggie?"

She wanted to tell them she wasn't going any further but she didn't have enough air for speech. She was walking backwards but all she could see was what lay ahead: the thick boughs she'd so often sat beneath, and the thin branches that draped down like whips. The leaves whispered when the wind blew and dragged ripples across water that was less than a metre deep. She'd drowned there all the same when the catfish dragged her away to watch TV.

"Hey." Fingers flapped clumsily against her face. "Are you hakking uit?"

"I don't know," she gasped. She was in her shield. She was safe in her shield because it meant nothing could get close enough to hurt her. She was safe, but she didn't feel safe because being invisible only protected her from outside things and Arno lived in her head with the narrator.

"Talk to me," Rob said, squeezing her hand. "Tell me what you're thinking."

"I drowned there. Puleng died there and the catfish made me watch it. The TV played endless repeats of the tick tock dog screaming and mascara lady becoming a speed bump when she tried to stop me from taking Mom's car, but no episode was the same. He was there in some of them."

"The telepath, Arno?"

She'd almost forgotten but now those memories rose from the murk, simultaneously brighter and blurrier. The episode where he spooned out the contents of her stomach and fed it to the tick tock dog, who was still whining for more when her gastric acid melted him from the inside out. The New Year's special where Arno mummified her in muddy plastic wrap so he could kiss her at midnight; his teeth scarifying her lips, his tongue like a fish's tail. Afterwards, he dipped his fist in oil and lit it. He laughed when he punched her and she became a Catherine Wheel, spinning across the sky, shedding sparks and chunks of flesh. Worst of all was the movie. His eyes glowed white in the dark, holding her gaze captive while he fucked Hachi in the dust and rubble littering the Waterfront Mall food court.

"I pretend she's you. I call her your name and make her forget it afterwards, but this could be real," he'd said, pulling Hachi's braid like a leash, spinning barbed wire from her hair to make a whip. "All you have to do is leave Enzo."

He raised his whip and safety pins held Maggie's eyes open and kept her screams caged. The escalator behind Arno and Hachi unravelled into a chainsaw which buzzed through the air, slicing her into a Maggie from before and a Maggie for after. She knew this because she'd run her fingers along the edges and sucked the blood off them afterwards. Blind monsters with greedy hands shlopped from the water and wormed inside to tongue Hachi's blood from the wounds where Arno flayed her. They rose and bowed at all the right times when Arno began to pray, panting to God and Maggie alike to love him. Maggie understood then that these monsters had lived inside him all along, that Arno had kept them hidden until that night. Their glowing eyes were a spotlight on her when Arno finished his benediction.

"All you have to do is love me." Arno looked at her with tears in his eyes. His monsters watched her too. They left streaks of Hachi's blood across their faces when they licked their lips.

"I don't want to remember." Maggie turned away from the line separating her from the rest of those memories.

"But we need to get you to Nico." Freddy resisted, holding her hand tightly but refusing to follow her.

"Nico can come to her," Rob said. "We'll find a place where you feel safe, Maggie, and you and Freddy can wait there while I speak to Enzo and Nico."

"Do I have to?" Freddy asked.

"Yes."

Maggie led them through buildings and over broken walls to the safety of the MTN shop in Nelson Mandela Drive. Glass crunched into the dust beneath her feet when she stepped through the broken door. When Freddy turned on a torch, the beam scattered around the room like a disco ball.

They watched the world until the bull-headed ostrich shadows in the parking lot turned syrupy. Now fluid, the shadows flowed into the darkness trapped beneath a minibus lying on its side. Maggie released her people then and Rob slipped out through the broken door.

"Stay with her," Rob said, and then he was gone.

The Complaints Procedure

The mould was breaking through her skin. It covered her in mottled green, black and white fur. It looked soft and plush, but Maggie didn't want to touch it because everyone knew mould was dangerous.

"...can't believe I have to wait here." Freddy paced behind her, each footstep a crunch of shattered glass and dust.

"With me?" Maggie bent to pick up a larger piece of glass from a corner of the room.

"In general. I hate waiting." He punctuated his words with a harsh scuff, a kick. "Would've been better if I went to speak to the people and Rob stayed here."

Maggie scraped the edge of the glass over her skin, removing the mould fur and some of the ugliness that prompted this growth spurt in the first place. She flicked it out through the maw where once the inside and outside were kept separate.

"What are you doing?"

"Removing the mould and the monsters. You should stay back so you don't breathe it in."

He didn't listen. His footsteps came up on her fast, followed by hands that folded over hers and lips that swore. He pried her fingers open to remove the glass.

"I'm still using that."

"For what? You're going to hurt yourself."

"The mould." She raised her arm so it was illuminated in the light from the torch he'd propped up on a chair. "Remembering the chainsaw has made it grow like crazy."

"You're not a piece of bread and there isn't any mould." The glass snapped and ground beneath his boot. His face was a weird consortium of twitching eye muscles and lines making rivers for disgust, confusion, pity.

"It's there." Maggie turned away from him. "It's usually underneath, but it grows between the stitches and sometimes it finds a way to the surface."

"There's no mould and no stitches!"

His shout passed through her like an earthquake. It trembled along the spike in her chest long after the initial tremor had exited via her feet. She touched her finger to the sharp tip until it stilled.

"You're too loud," she muttered.

Freddy groaned. "I haven't got the krag for this now. I'm going out for a bit."

"You can't."

His face was mostly in shadow but she saw his jaw clench tight and a muscle jumped beneath his right eye.

"I need space before I get bevok, Maggie," he said.

"It's dangerous." She snatched at his hand. "There's leopards and dogs and buffalo, and hands with long fingers that grab you and lick you."

He held his right hand out to the side. Maggie watched his fingers fuse together and his wrist widen. His forearm lost its colour, turning silvery and flattening until all the flesh beyond his elbow was a blade.

"I can take care of myself," Freddy said. "I was being mugged when the Change happened."

He stood and his forearm returned to meat and bone as quickly as it had become metal. She watched him stride away until the night swallowed him. He shouldn't be out there alone, knife arms or not. A multitude of insects sang and screamed outside and for a while she could track Freddy's movement by listening for where they turned silent, but then there wasn't any more silence. There was time instead, ticking and chattering, a little dog that never went away. Maggie reached for her spear, but it wasn't here.

Time was eating through the air conditioning pipes. She followed the sound of blunt nails scraping on thin metal up the stairs.

There was a floor in a room of the upper level of the building that was carpeted with bats. Wings outstretched, overlapping, they'd mummified into a solid being of many grimacing heads. Their eyes reflected Maggie's torchlight back at her, green and red. Teeth chattered, straining for her ankles as she tiptoed across them. Maybe this was what she'd heard, not time.

A skeleton waited for her behind the far door. It lounged in one of those fancy, extra comfy office chairs, coffee mug close at hand, computer screen positioned at an angle on one corner of the desk.

"Dumela, goeie aand, good evening, how can I help you today?"

Maggie hesitated. The skeleton's 'dealing with the public' voice was just false enough to betray an undercurrent of irritation, but she was here now and she had to follow through.

"I have a complaint," Maggie said.

"Please take a seat and tell me the nature of your complaint."

"I'm not happy with the way things have been going lately." Maggie lowered herself into one of the chairs opposite the skeleton. "Actually, I haven't been happy with the way things have been going for a long while but it's been especially bad the past few days."

"This is an existential complaint then?" Phalanges click-clacked across the keyboard and the skeleton turned its empty eye sockets toward the screen.

"I'm not sure."

"Existential complaints deal with your basic existence and how satisfied you are with it."

"Definitely an existential complaint then."

The skeleton tapped a few more keys and uhmed and ahhed at the screen. Maggie looked around the office, noting a small family photo of two women and three kids, and a certificate hanging skew on the wall. The name on the certificate was Sincerity.

"Okay, miss, what exactly is the problem you've encountered?"

"It's complicated. I don't like how people keep doing stuff and telling me things like I'm supposed to know what's true and what's unreality. It's fucking frustrating, and then they act like they have more right to be annoyed about it than I do! What the fuck is that?"

"That is the basic nature of people, miss," Sincerity replied. "Empathy is in short supply but self-interest is bountiful. This office cannot accept complaints based purely on the drawbacks of having to deal with other humans on a daily basis. Your complaint has to be directly related to the Apocalypse and events surrounding it."

"And it is." Maggie leaned forward. "Things wouldn't be this bad if Arno hadn't tortured me, and he wouldn't have been able to do that if he hadn't gotten a telepathy power during the Apocalypse."

"Then this is an SGA complaint. Why did you say it was existential?"

"What is an SGA?"

"Supernatural Gained Ability." Sincerity peered at her from the other side of the desk. "Miss, I can't help you unless you provide clear and accurate information."

"I'm trying."

Sincerity shook her head, tapped at the keyboard again. "I'm going to print an SGA complaint form for you." Sincerity spun away on her office chair to retrieve the form from a dust-laden printer. "Once you've completed the form, I'll show you where to sign and initial."

"I guess that's okay."

Sincerity spun back a few moments later and plopped the freshly printed pages in front of Maggie along with a pen.

Maggie immediately started filling in questions. Twenty-three years later, her hand was cramped into a rigid claw, but she was finished. She gathered the pages together and handed them to Sincerity.

"Let's see now..." Sincerity extended her pointer finger, the bones hovering just above the page. "You haven't filled in the ID number of the person you're complaining about."

"Because I don't know his ID number. I'm not even sure what mine was."

Sincerity made a disapproving sound. She tapped her finger at another blank spot on the form. "You haven't filled in how this person manifested their SGA either."

"Because I don't know." Maggie leaned forward until the edge of the desk pressed against her ribs. Black threads had gathered where Sincerity's finger made contact with the page. They bled from the ink in filaments thinner than cotton thread, winding over the blank spaces between words and answers she didn't have to tap at Sincerity's yellowing bones.

"This is crucial information, miss," Sincerity continued. "If you can't describe the circumstances under which the SGA manifestation occurred then we can't establish whether this person underwent a negative manifestation or not."

"What's that supposed to mean?"

Sincerity folded her hands together and rested them on the form. A few inky threads attached to her bones.

"SGA that manifested during negative experiences results in individuals gaining dangerous powers and an antisocial outlook. These people are prone to violence and delusional episodes."

Maggie blinked, and in that tiny moment, the threads attached to Sincerity's bones multiplied. They crisscrossed like untidy spider webs, travelled across bone like veins.

"People generally refer to them as *crazies* or *malkoppe*. You've probably encountered at least one of these dangerous SGAs before."

"Ja, the one I'm complaining about," Maggie replied.

"So you say, but we can't establish that unless you provide the necessary information. See, you don't even have a certified proof of address for this person."

"How would I get that? We live in an Apocalypse, and even if we didn't, how can you expect me to provide proof of address for someone who attacked me?"

"We need the information for the system. ID number,

proof of address, a signed affidavit from the person confirming that they caused you harm, a photographic portfolio of head and full body shots that includes swimwear, dental records and a COVID vaccination certificate."

Maggie stared at Sincerity. Her brain bubbled and fizzed with the impossibility of what the skeleton was asking of her. She followed the tracks of the threads winding up her ulna, webbing over her humerus.

"The complaint can be filed without this information, but it will be marked incomplete and will take longer to process."

"How much longer?"

Sincerity made a back and forth motion with her hand in the air, threads trailing like void-dark gossamer. "Fifteen million years."

"This is the most fucked-up thing I've ever heard." Maggie slammed her palm down on the desk. "What's the point of laying a complaint if you won't do anything about it?"

"Of course we will, I just told you so."

"In fifteen million years' time. That's super helpful."

"There's no need for attitude, miss. We can only do so much if you're unable to provide accurate information."

"So you're saying it's my fault you're inefficient?"

"Exactly."

The outline of lips were forming around Sincerity's teeth. All across her skull, the black threads had interposed themselves like the lines of an artist's sketch. When Maggie glanced down at the form, it was blank. Every question printed on the page was gone, as well as all the information she'd filled in. Rage scraped against the inside hollow of her ribs. Her eyes prickled with tears. She ripped away the top pages of the form, revealing even more blank pages beneath, and balled them up in her fist.

Sincerity started to object when Maggie climbed onto the desk, but Maggie crammed the balled paper between her outline lips. Several of Sincerity's teeth fell out, clinking onto the desk, bouncing to the floor, skipping up Maggie's forearm while she grabbed more pages to shove between Sincerity's jaws.

She was swearing and crying, but couldn't hear herself doing it. Small lights formed in Sincerity's eye sockets, growing brighter until Maggie couldn't bear to look at them. She shut her eyes, but those lights blazing from Sincerity's skull were burned into her retinas in shades of purple and red. Her right knee slipped. Her ribs crashed against a sharp edge and then she was tumbling for a lifetime through space before landing on her back.

Someone chuckled—not Sincerity. The sound was deep and a little throaty.

"I think I like you, Maggie," he said.

"Who cares?" She rolled onto her side, ignoring the spear of pain down her spine.

"You should. It's not often I find lesser creatures endearing."

Maggie blinked rapidly. The afterimage of Sincerity's burning eye sockets was fading, visible only as a vague shape superimposed over the filthy floor.

"Who are you to decide that I'm lesser?"

The man laughed again. Maggie knelt and turned towards the sound. A dark figure stood before the floor to ceiling windows, silhouetted against the red light of dawn.

"I am the maker of all that you are, all that you see." He stretched out his arms. Sincerity's ribs were still visible beneath the tangled threads covering his chest. "I am the mother who birthed all your fervent wishes into reality and the father of shadows. I am—"

"You're that origin dude Rob told me about."

The shadow man's hands curled into fists. "I was at the beginning of a glorious speech that elucidates all questions your teensy mortal mind could hold and you just butt right in. Rude. Disrespectful." He stuck a hand out at Maggie, arm like a pole, and shadow threads burst from his fingers. They stuck to Maggie's shoulders and chest, lifting her from the floor to dangle in front of him.

"Die."

Bargains

The origin shadow's voice reverberated off the walls and set the glass panes in the window quivering. It was the same earaching noise of a sound system with shot speakers and the bass set too high. His eyes glowed white, as did the gaps between his teeth when he smiled at Maggie. Vibrations pulsed down the threads attached to her flesh, sending painful concussive waves into her that shook the mould spores free and made her belly ache. A house party crashed along her veins, rending the walls to tatters that flapped and tickled. Thoughts she'd packed neatly into boxes burst open, spilling down the water slides and sticking to the walls like movie posters. Rob's face was on one of them, telling her she could banish this creature, the origin of shadows, that she'd done it in his visions countless times.

She still hadn't seen the end of that movie, didn't know what would happen next, but the potentials for afterwards were here nonetheless. Fighting was how she'd keep her new people so she tugged her invisibility shield on. It dimmed the pain, but the shadow man was still there, his threads still stuck to her skin. The light between his teeth grew brighter.

"You have the nerve to use one of the powers I granted your kind against me?" he snarled.

"I'm supposed to." Maggie reached out with her legs and found purchase on Sincerity's chair. "I'm meant to defeat you."

"Defeat me?" The shadow man made a sound like a cat bringing up a hairball. "I am your benefactor, you ungrateful lump of meat. Without me you have no powers, no magic, nothing but ruins—"

"What?" Maggie's foot slipped on the chair. "What do you mean no powers?"

The shadow man's skin was jiggling now, sending out spikes that speared through the floating dust motes and receded in the time it took to blink. That must be the same as what was happening inside her now with the vibrations and the mould.

"I birthed your abilities. If you vanish me with your power then you'll lose it forever."

Rob never mentioned that. The information shook through her bones and blood in counterpoint to the tremors caused by the shadow man's threads. It muddied the water slides and the thoughts perched atop them with nausea, set the catfish writhing. Maggie was but seconds from rattling apart in a spray of atoms, but she needed to think, to act, something.

"You didn't know that." The shadow man was shaking so hard now it looked like there were three of him. "Not selfless then, but ignorant. Stop your attack and I'll stop mine. I'll tell you the truth your master has hidden from you."

"I have no master."

"Your sender. The one who misled you."

Had Rob misled her? It didn't seem like something he'd do on purpose but maybe, maybe. All her muscles pulled tight as a particularly powerful vibration caught on her spine, a pain beyond screaming. Rob's earnestness and empathy stuck in her chest. Were they really her people?

"So you'd rather die for their lies?"

"No." Maggie locked her gaze on the origin shadow. Oil slick shimmers of purple, red and green reflected across the black puddle surrounding his feet. "I want to know what's real."

Maggie partially released her shield. The shadow man pulled back on several threads connected to her shoulders and chest, leaving bruised skin and bleeding pinpricks behind. He might lie, but he might tell her the truth, or perhaps she'd realise there was a gap between what Rob knew and things Rob didn't know that he didn't know. By degrees, Maggie and the shadow man released each other, until the world no longer shook.

"My power, everyone's power, depends on you?" Maggie asked.

The shadow man grimaced. "Why would you expect otherwise when I am the sole reason they exist?"

"But why give us powers in the first place?" she continued. "Why do any of this?"

The light in his eyes flickered. "Your powers are an unforeseen side-effect, a mistake, if you will, or a happy accident. Those who summoned me to this pocket of existence wished for the power to alter existence and I had to comply. The result was all of this."

Maggie sat on Sincerity's chair. This was all too big for her skull and her boxes were a mess. "You caused the Apocalypse because some dudes summoned you to give them power?"

"I am a creator with a desire to serve. I also did not have much choice in the matter. There I was, peacefully tending the interstitial pathways between realities, when my true name thundered along the rainbows, compelling me into the midst of your type, meat-beings." He flapped his fingers at her. "I provided the magical power source to fuel their grand intent, but they failed to specify that this ability to change should be nested within their meat, nor did they define the exact nature of the change they desired." He gave an exaggerated shrug. "You'd think beings capable of summoning me here would know magic requires specific intent to achieve best results, but no. I couldn't even tidy it up because of the way they summoned me, into a guarded circle, of all things, so I powered the spell and it backfired."

"And that meant some of us got powers and the rest died?"

"Everyone who was wishing and hoping for something with all their soul manifested a power based on that wish. I believe the magic was seeking direction, a way to fulfil its purpose of effecting change, and that was provided by creatures like you."

Her power was nothing but a random accident then, a product of a monumental screw-up and her desperation to get away from the mascara lady and the ache of her empty home, her wish to get rid of her problems by disappearing.

"And the shadows?"

"Propagated from the teeth of those who summoned me." His bright grin widened. "They did not survive the change they requested, unfortunately. I had to punish them for making such a mess, and then I had to do something to fix the balance, so I picked their teeth from the chewy bits and set them to work on doing just that. The result is interesting."

The way he referred to it as 'the change' lodged between the two meridians of Maggie's brain. Had Rob asked her to destroy the shadows while knowing that would destroy her powers too? Everyone's powers. What chance did she have of getting better if she removed the powers of the person who might be able to heal her? Had that been his plan, to promise her salvation while knowing he'd never have to stick to it?

No, the plan had been healing then Joburg. This encounter was a spanner fallen amidst the gears and cogs.

"I'll make you a deal."

The shadow man was difficult to look at, an utter darkness with limned features set against the backdrop of golden sunlight.

"You like having power, and without me you have none. Your sender either lied to you about the consequences of challenging me, or they are not as wise as they've led you to believe. It seems to me you've been cheated."

She hated him for summarising her feelings so succinctly. The balloon was still there, still floated in her chest but now it was more like a wrinkled thing one might find on the side of the road, a balloon that had escaped a kid's party and now was as lost as she was. She'd trusted Rob's confidence about his visions, and he'd been wrong. The things he did n't know about the shadow man could fill the Mariana Trench, and his guesswork was just dangerous.

"I don't need the sales pitch," Maggie muttered. "Just tell me your offer."

The shadow man's eyes narrowed to twin slits of light. "Your rudeness is going to get you killed. Not today, probably, not by me. This time, I will let you go and, in return, you won't interfere with my presence in this corner of existence."

"That's a shitty offer. You think I don't know that the only reason we're talking at all right now is because I was actually hurting you? That I believe you're all kind and want to be nice to me?" Maggie shook her head. He was just like a person, and people were monsters. "If you want me to let you go, I want you to make me better."

He didn't speak or move. The only sign he'd heard her were the small needles of oil slick darkness rippling across his skin.

"Do you not value your life?" he asked.

"Not if everyone I meet betrays me. Why... I'd rather be dead than alone."

"I can do dead for you." He moved closer, hands out as though he were going to hug her, but threads writhed along his fingers. "I can even make it quick."

"I'd rather die fighting."

His shoulders slumped and his hands dropped. "Fine. I'll grant you a favour, because I pity you, and only if it's a small one. There are still a lot of messy side-effects I need to tidy up in this existence before I can implement the redesign and reconnect the pathways, and it's taken too long already. Define exactly how you're unwell. Unless you're specific, the bargain is forfeit."

Ice-cold panic poured over her head and set like concrete in her guts. She'd have to explain about the mould, about the stitches and the seams, the slides and boxes, the catfish. Whenever she tried to explain to people they looked through her and beyond, to places where flowers grew and frolicking happened. She couldn't provide a cognitive frame of reference to span the distance from frolicking to water slides! It could make everything worse if she tried, and being worse than she was now would be the end of her. Her only option was to work sideways.

"What if I wished for more power, or to alter a power in a specific way?"

"Interesting." The origin tipped his head to one side. "Yes, that might count as a small wish."

"Then I wish for Rob and Freddy's healer friend, Nico,

to have the ability to heal psychological damage, all forms of mental health disorders, any neurological, psychological or other mental wounds, including those caused by other abilities, no matter what the nature of the ability or damage it causes... and that healing such wounds will be as easy for him to do as healing any physical wound."

"You're using your favour to augment somebody else's power?"

"Yes."

"Without their consent?"

"Does that matter?"

"Of course." He bent forward at the waist. "Anything done to someone else without their agreement can be assumed to be unwelcome. You should know this; after all, you were altered without your consent. Would you wish to hold the hand that punched you moments before?"

Maggie shook her head. "It's not the same. I was attacked, but wishing for Nico to have a permanent power upgrade is a good thing. It will benefit him and probably lots of other people too, not just me."

"Probably, but the terms and conditions rule everything." His grin was like a sickle moon. "It's a guarantee that causes and effects will balance perfectly, Maggie. Are you sure this is what you want?"

"Yes."

The shadow man touched his thumb and pointer finger together. "There, it's done. Customer satisfaction is not guaranteed. Terms and conditions apply."

"What about refunds and exchanges?"

But the shadow man just smiled and waved at her. He was melting. Black strings dripped from his form to the floor, revealing Sincerity's bones. They were whiter than they had been and cracked and snapped when they landed in the growing pool of darkness on the floor. Maggie moved closer, but warded off the temptation to scoop some onto her fingers and lick it. The liquid oozed up the glass and squeezed between several thin cracks Maggie hadn't noticed before. She had to tilt her head to watch it flow along the narrow concrete ledge outside, and then it was gone.

"I'm sorry to inform you that the system is offline, miss, so we can't process your complaint."

Maggie jumped and whirled around. Sincerity was back, her skull balanced precariously against her scapula on one side and the top vertebrae of her neck on the other.

"Please come back next year and we will assist you then," Sincerity continued.

"To hell with your system." Maggie grabbed Sincerity's skull from the heap of bones and smashed it against the wall. Her lower jaw fell free and landed near Maggie's feet.

Maggie squatted and ran her finger along the teeth that remained on Sincerity's jaw. Hope and something else, something spiny as a sea urchin, moved inside her. Terms and conditions be damned. She could be better now the origin had granted her wish, like the Maggie she was before, but first she needed to face Rob and Freddy.

This was an afterwards she hadn't anticipated. Maggie wiggled a loose molar. But maybe she was thinking about everything wrong. She could glide over facing Rob and Freddy without them knowing this was the afterwards and get healed by their friend first. Then she'd have made a new afterwards and a new before version of herself. That was the answer; Maggie felt it in her mud and marrow. Exactly how it would make a difference remained elusive but Maggie saw no option but to trust to her intuition.

The tooth popped free and Maggie rolled it into her palm. She also had to find out if Rob had lied to her, if he'd known she'd lose her powers when she killed the origin. If he had... they couldn't be her people if he had, and then what would she do?

"Maggie!"

Maggie turned and rose just as Freddy appeared through the door at the far end of the room.

"Thank God you're here. Come quickly," he turned to go back the way he'd come. "There's something going on and I'm scared Rob is in trouble."

One Afterwards of Many

Shadows swarmed the street outside, more than Maggie had ever seen in one place. There were porcupine hyenas and giraffe-necked hippos with cheetah tails. Jackals crowned with buffalo horns wove between the legs of elephants with multiple crocodile tails sprouting from their rears.

"It's a parade," Maggie said. The shadows must've gathered to put on a show for the origin.

"That's why I need you to cover me, make me invisible."

Maggie looked at him askance. "For what?"

"I heard people shouting and now they're quiet." He frowned, shifting his weight from one foot to the other. "We need to find out what's happening, if Rob and Nico got cornered out there."

"How does random shouting add up to Rob and Nico being in trouble?"

"It means someone's in trouble, and that someone might be them."

The logic was flawed. She couldn't imagine anyone would be dumb enough to take a stroll in the daylight, but there was shining desperation in his big eyes and chewed lips. She might still want to keep these people as hers and that meant helping him.

"Where did you hear them?"

"That way." He pointed down the street.

If Rob and Nico had exited the zoo from the front of the hotel then they might've crossed the old parking area which connected the two streets.

"I'll go and take a look."

"I'm coming with you. There's no time to argue," he added when she turned to look at him.

Maggie took his hand and shrugged away the world. Together, they strode across to a line of trees growing near the road and followed them down.

"When did you get back?" Maggie asked, as they waited for a river of rat-sized shadows pouring down the overgrown paving leading from an underground parking area to the street.

"Just before dawn," he whispered. "Should we be talking? Won't they hear us?"

"I don't think they hear anything," Maggie replied. "What you really have to worry about is something smelling us."

Freddy made a guttural sound that might've been a suppressed cough or a growl.

The last of the small shadows passed. Maggie stepped over the short wall and followed them down to the street. Freddy bumped against her as the crowd of shadows swelled outwards, almost touching them. He stayed there, warm, wiry and shivering against her side. Fear. Of course he was afraid; he wasn't like her.

Maggie pulled him after her until they reached the edge of the parking lot outside the bank. Some of the covered parking still stood. Freddy moved ahead and into the shade of the closest one.

"The zoo hotel is just over there, in the next street," Maggie said. "If someone came from that side, they probably crossed here."

"I haven't seen anyone."

"I'm shrugging. I know you can't see it so I'm telling you."

"I felt it," he said. "I think we should go in there."

It was cooler inside the building than out, but not by much. It smelled like rodents and growled like dogs yet there was something profoundly, fundamentally wrong with the everything of this situation. She stabbed at the fish swimming beneath the dust and muck coating the walls with her fingernails. Something with eyelids blinked at her from beneath a lily pad. Trash collected in an eddy. Why would someone paint a mural of her mind? The sleek skin of a catfish broke the surface briefly.

"Don't just stand there, help me search," Freddy said.

"Why?" Maggie lunged for the catfish but missed. "This whole thing doesn't make sense and why am I helping you anyway?"

Freddy was three doors further down the corridor. He looked back at her now, deadpan.

"You were kinda mean to me last night, weren't you? The type of mean that's been suppressed and squeezes out like toothpaste when shit gets real."

"I was frustrated. I... do you have any idea how weird it is for me to be staying with a... person like you." He came toward her with big, stomping footsteps. "I've been nearly crushed by some fucking Scraptimus Prime thing and locked in a dog cage by a lady who wanted to feed me to her parrots. Now there's you." He looked her up and down. "You were supposed to be our salvation. Finding you was supposed to be step one on the road to making everything better, but then we got here and you're like... like all the crazies who've tried to kill me before, but also not. And I don't know what to think about you."

"I didn't think parrots ate meat," she said, because it was true and because his angry words made something hurt in her balloon. The mould itched along her ribs and that spiny, sea urchin feeling was velcroing itself to her intestines.

"This is what I mean." He ran his hands over his head. "I say something and you come back with something that's so... why, from all of that, is the parrots the thing you grab onto?"

"Because they're herbivores, aren't they?" Maggie hung her head.

He dropped his hands to his hips and she heard him huff. This was the truth of Freddy, she realised: impatient, insensitive and incapable of dealing with people when he wasn't actively manipulating them to kill his monsters.

"Never mind, none of this matters right now. I don't see signs that anyone's been in here recently, so where else might they be?"

Back to his illogical hunt for random shouty people. A narcissistic diversion. She watched weeds rising to the surface in the mural, greenery broken by slick, dark ripples of catfish. They were spawning.

"You would've liked the Maggie I was in the before, before." She looked up at Freddy. "Everyone thought she was so much fun. They came to my parties and laughed about how I stole the booze and told mascara lady to get lost when she complained about the noise. You might even have been friends with her but she would've eaten you alive then blocked you. I actually value people, but only so long as they value me."

"What's that supposed to mean? You think I don't value people?"

Away. He shouted after her but she didn't want to be here anymore. One step then three, five turned to ten. She reached the foyer and Freddy was still behind, where she left him, not following with claws or apologies but staring after her with those red eyes. She told herself it didn't matter and that the things he'd said weren't still bleeding inside of her. A zebra wa-wa-wa'ed somewhere distant, dogs barked and birds chirped. A serpent circled the sun and the shadows were still gathered in the streets like drunkards after a rugby match.

All she had to do now was find Rob and Nico and then she'd be healed. They weren't outside in the stupid sun, they were at the zoo. Freddy had been lying to her, trying to keep her from being okay again. Had he seen her talking to the origin? Did he overhear her making a bargain with him?

Maggie looked back at the open doors behind her. It didn't matter if he knew—he was stranded here now, and would remain stranded until the sun faded and took the shadows with it.

A strange calmness netted the catfish, trapping them in a membrane beneath the mud. There was a short way that she should've taken before when she was leading Rob and Freddy here. It didn't go past the water or the willow trees where Arno's ghost lived. It wasn't polite to visit through the back door, not unless you were very good friends with the people you were visiting, but Maggie was above and orbiting far beyond such details. Manners were just the string on a kite, a tether she needed to slip free of now to save herself.

Freddy would like her once she was healed. They could be friends then; he could still be one of her people. If she wanted him. She might even be able to return to the zoo, to carry on her life there. They'd take her back if she was okay, why wouldn't they? She'd be able to choose which people she preferred to keep, but that was a task for the after Maggie. Right now there were other bridges to cross and rivers to swim.

Someone was shouting, just like Freddy said, but it was coming from the zoo.

Terms and Conditions

The zoo hotel was concerned. Shadows licked at its eyes and scrabbled against its thick grey skin, pulling down wrinkles they used as ladders. They parted for Maggie's shield and were pulled into the gravity of her emptiness. Shadows circled her like a drain as she approached the hotel's screaming gullet.

Somebody's empty skin and clothes lay across the step before the former main entrance, now the back door. Face-down and floppy, Maggie couldn't tell which one of her former people had sacrificed themselves to become a welcome mat so she poked it with her foot, waited to see if it would bite. It flopped and skidded a little when the hotel inhaled, and again when it released fresh shouts, bays and howls from the voices inside it. Maggie still wasn't a good enough friend anymore to enter through the back but this was urgent, so she hopped over the welcome skin and into the hotel's throat.

Chunky, concrete puzzle pieces littered the manicured lawn spread across the floor and one of the doors leading to the dining room had leapt from its hinges to trap a child's plastic kick bike. Bibi's plastic kick bike, unless other children had happened in the time she'd been gone. A yellow mongoose bounded from the dining room with screams in its teeth. It ran circles and spirals across the grass then disappeared behind the reception desk while the bike's pink wheels spun in the air, searching for traction.

Maggie approached the bike. "It's okay, I'll help you."

The bike's wheels spun faster, and faster still when she gripped the edge of the door holding it down.

"You don't need to be afraid of me. I know my shield makes you feel icky but I'm going to help you."

Maggie lifted the door and set it aside. A gunshot boomed down the staircase to her left, followed by a throat-shredding howl. The kick bike startled and raced away across the foyer without thanking her. Two springboks skidded and tumbled down the stairs, limbs knotting then releasing, knotting then releasing. A shrunken elephant followed on their heels. All three started for the kitchen with the fluidity of a herd driven by a singular purpose, and they stopped like one too when they reached the edge of Maggie's shield.

"You guys feel that?" the elephant asked.

"Feels like..." the first springbok said.

"Maggie," said the second springbok.

Maggie studied the trio under a microscope but there was nothing familiar about any of them, except for their voices, perhaps. Somewhere around the furthest corners of her mind a bell laughed with a voice very much like the second springbok, and another swore with the elephant's gruff timbre, but the echoes were confusing.

"Hi, I am Maggie. I'm looking for Rob, have any of you seen..."

Maggie didn't finish because the animals were out of earshot now, and out of sight beyond the walls keeping the dining room in a static place. The clattering of the springboks' hooves and the elephant's trumpeting lingered on the air in their wake and sent shock waves into the mud. Something that wasn't a catfish stirred beneath the surface; a leech, or an eel with throats in throats in throats and teeth lining all of them. Maggie fed it the words she didn't get to speak and started up the stairs. It made sense to start searching for Rob from top to bottom so she could use the upper floors as a vantage point. Also, if Freddy had heard him screaming then it was logical that he'd be in the place where everyone else was screaming, and that place was upstairs.

A honey badger, a duiker and a twirling table passed her on the stairs. The latter smashed against the wall above the landing and hit Maggie with one of its legs. There was more screaming, and more animals sweating against her, pushing and bruising, and gone. It was bedlam, except bedlam was a description originating from a mental hospital with the same name so she was bedlam and this was something else. Maybe this wasn't the best place to start searching for Rob after all, but she was already at the top of the stairs now, dodging a 'flying' Enzo.

He'd only recently started "flying lessons" if his messy landing was anything to go by. He hit the wall neck first and let out a cry so plaintive and pain-filled that Maggie almost stopped to help him. But he was a lying, betraying asshole so she turned away to study a spray of blood across the wall. A smear intersected it, like the artist had been unsatisfied with the result and dragged their hand through it. Beside it, claws had gouged furrows through the plaster and into the brick beneath, exposing worms to the light, pointing to the shadowed end of the hallway where a scarecrow was pointing a gun at a golden angel with bald wings.

Well, that would explain why Enzo's flying lessons were going badly—feathery wings didn't work if they were bald.

The scarecrow fired the gun and the angel recoiled from the impact, falling backwards, leaving a spray of golden dust in her wake as she cartwheeled through an open door. Maybe they worked like butterfly wings instead, somehow reliant on their covering of dust to defy gravity. The scarecrow yelled and fired again, and again, but you couldn't kill angels with bullets and why would anyone try? Angels were good, and they were messengers too. You weren't supposed to shoot the messenger but maybe the scarecrow didn't know that because he had no brain.

The angel tackled the scarecrow. Maggie tried to peer around them as they grappled to see if Rob was somewhere in the hallway beyond them but they flailed too much. Although she didn't want to people, they left her no choice.

Maggie edged closer. "Excuse me, you're blocking the passage."

They rudely ignored her. Maggie cleared her throat and tried again: "Could you move, please? I need to get past."

The angel bit the scarecrow's wrist and he roared, pressed the muzzle of the gun against the angel's side, and shot her. Her wings jerked open with a spray of dust that stung Maggie's eyes. They were way too involved in their own business to pay her any mind. The only way past them was to join their violence. Maggie didn't know whose side to pick or what they were fighting about so she listened to the theme music. Violins shrieked when the angel slashed at the scarecrow with her claws but it was overshadowed by triumphant drums when he knocked her legs out from under her. Horns blared when he straightened his arms, aiming at her head, and collapsed into evil electronica laughs when the angel rolled away.

Maggie knew what to do. She pushed the scarecrow aside when the angel leapt at him and felt her face jerk when claws hooked through the flesh. Momentum separated them, but Maggie went back for her. She hugged the angel's throat from behind, holding onto her with all her might while she screamed and rent the wall. Her wings beat at Maggie's ribs and her nails scraped through the mould covering the bones in her arms, but she only needed to hold on for four minutes. Unless angels didn't need to breathe.

They went through a wall and a door and broke one of the hotel's eyes, releasing a beam of sunlight that glittered across the dust from the angel's wings. Then Maggie was sitting on a bookcase with the angel flailing in her arms. She hugged her with her legs too then, and they tumbled to the floor. The edge of the bookcase scraped down Maggie's spine and threw her forward. Her teeth met skull and tangled hair. Another gunshot set her ears ringing and sprayed splinters from the desk in front of them.

"Stop shooting, you moron," Maggie shouted. She grabbed the angel's hair and pulled her neck back, remembered the movie where Arno did this to Hachi and then pushed the memory into the mud, and put all her weight behind smashing the angel's face into the carpet. Angel wings almost unseated her, flailing and flapping, beating her blue and clogging the air with glitter. It took twenty-two and a half smashes before the angel went still.

Maggie stroked the angel's hair. It was matted into filthy worms, but Maggie massaged glitter into it to make her hair pretty before she gathered it at the nape of her neck with shaking fingers. She tried to wipe away the blood leaking down her arms and dripping from her head onto the angel's tattered dress and dirty skin, but that only made it worse. Next, she straightened out the angel's wings. All the glitter was gone from them now and the bare skin beneath was covered in scabs and raw patches that weeped. Maggie was careful not to touch them in case the angel was diseased.

When she finished, Maggie rose and straightened out the angel's dress. She sighed away her shield and stared into the barrel of a gun.

"Vanish and I'll shoot you."

The scarecrow's brown eyes glared at her from beyond the gun. Blood streaked his face too.

"Hi, I'm just here to look for Rob and Nico," Maggie said.

"Ja, sure. I'll tell them you were looking for them but you're not staying here. Go back to the hole you crawled from, they'll find you there."

Maggie wiped away the blood flowing across her right eye. Were all scarecrows this hostile? Why had the theme music implied he was the good guy when he was an asshole?

"Loop." He gestured with his head towards the door.

"Why are you so rude?" Maggie stepped over the angel.

"Do you really expect me to be nice to you?" Dust and fine bits of straw sprayed from the scarecrow's mouth as he made a guttural sound of disgust. "I know exactly what you're capable of, Maggie, and I'll put a hole in your head before I let you hurt anyone here."

"You talk like you know me, but if you did then you'd know that I wouldn't hurt anyone in the zoo."

"Just go!" He circled around, herding her towards the door. "This is fucking malkop bullshit; take it with you and get out. One more word of it and I'm shooting you."

Maggie recoiled. Had she made a mistake? Was the scarecrow not the good guy?

A rooikat bounded through the door before she reached it and skidded to a stop, claws digging into the carpet.

"Where's the crazy?" the rooikat asked in a feminine voice.

"Over there. I think it's dead," the scarecrow replied.

The rooikat looked Maggie in the eye then, flattened its sharp ears and bared its teeth. "What's she doing here?"

"Murder. Will you check that thing's unalived? I'm getting Maggie out of here before she attacks us too."

"Why would I do that?" Maggie said.

"Because you're a crazy, just like that thing with the scabby wings was."

"Fuck you." Maggie turned to the scarecrow. "You don't even know me."

"Jesus, Maggie." The scarecrow glanced past her, to the rooikat. "Hachi and I know you very fucking well."

"Hachi?" Maggie locked gazes with the rooikat and moved closer. "What happened to you? Did Arno do this?"

The rooikat hissed at her. "Don't ever say that name to me."

"Out of here, now." The scarecrow pushed her towards the door.

Maggie stepped out into the passage with the scarecrow just behind her. "If that's what Hachi looks like now, then who are you?"

"It's Luan, you weirdo."

She glanced back at him and it sort of made sense. Luan had always been into weapons and defences and scarecrows, brainless and silly as they were, were guardians.

"I don't understand." She wasn't feeling too good now and had to lean against the wall to navigate across some chunks of broken wall and furniture. "Why would you become a scarecrow instead of a sentry turret, or a guard dog?"

"Hou jou bek," the scarecrow muttered behind her. "And keep walking. You're bleeding on everything."

Maggie stopped then and looked down at herself. There was quite a lot of blood on her arms and hands, one side of her belly and the top part of her chest. It was mostly the congealing type of blood though.

"Keep moving." The scarecrow prodded her between her shoulder blades.

Maggie moved forwards, towards the ribbons of green and pink light stretched across the entrance to the stairs. A man with the Aurora Australis combing through his curly dark hair crouched there beside Enzo's legs.

"Hey, Nico. This one was looking for you," Scarecrow Luan called out.

The man glanced over his shoulder. This was Nico? Her salvation had a plush toy softness about him that made her rush towards him, made her open her arms to cuddle the stuffing out of him. But then there was a whine and limbs danced in warning. Past Nico's squishy shoulder, Enzo stared at her like she'd stepped out of a horror movie wearing pale make-up and carrying a panga. He pressed himself into the wall until it covered him like a tortoise shell and Maggie heard guitar strings snapping inside of her.

First there was scarecrow Luan, then Hachi the rooikat and now Enzo was becoming a tortoise. There was no way she could come back to these people when they were all evolving into something inhuman, something potentially inhumane if it was a transformation birthed in fear and an eagerness to shoot her. They were changing, and she would be changing too but it seemed unlikely that their respective befores and afters would harmonise. Scarecrow Luan wouldn't even let her stay to find Rob, even after she'd trusted the theme music and killed an angel.

She knew then that she could never be part of this community like she was before. They might be happy to let her fetch and carry and explore under the cover of her invisibility but then they'd leave her at the gate like a servant, lock her out like a dog. That wouldn't do. She'd rather take her chances with the new people.

"You must be Maggie. I thought..." Nico frowned. "Is Freddy here too?"

Maggie shook her head. Galaxies spiraled in his eyes and she had to squint into his gaze . "He's safe, he's—"

"You can catch up later," Luan said and prodded her again. "She's not staying."

"But she's hurt," Nico replied.

"Not badly."

"Still. You're not taking her anywhere until I've healed her."

Nico reached out to her with no hesitation, no fluctuation, no wavering of intent. He wasn't even the least bit afraid of her. Maggie watched his advancing hands but found she wasn't afraid of him either.

"Can, can you—" Maggie whispered.

His smile revealed a dimple stitched into his cheek. "Rob told me you need my help, but right now, I'm just going to heal these wounds, okay?"

He watched her while he wiped at her arms with a cloth, waiting, waiting for something from her. The furthest arms of his galaxies hooked into question marks but Maggie didn't know the answers to questions that size.

"Is that okay Maggie?"

"What?"

"I'm going to heal these wounds now and later on we'll see if there's anything I can do for your mental wounds."

"Okay."

He nodded, and the aurora poured down from his head to cloak his shoulders. He raised his hand to hover near her face and Maggie resisted the urge to squeeze his stuffing by balling her hands into fists, clenching her jaw, forcing herself to be still, still, still, so still she could be confused for death. She wanted to burn in the stars spinning through his eyes and scoop up the celestial light in his hair so she could pour it down the water slides, but she could be patient first.

The stuffing under Nico's skin shifted, transforming his face from a placid blank to something frowny. He narrowed his eyes and clenched his jaw, looked to his hand, looked back to her. Something was wrong.

Luan laughed. "Maybe you can't heal crazies."

"What?"

Nico shook his head and reached out to her again. Again, he pulled back and glared at his hand. "I don't understand."

"Maybe you're tired?" Enzo stood behind him, leaving a cavity in the wall where the bricks and cement in his tortoise shell had once been.

"It doesn't work like that," Nico said.

"What's happening?"

Nico looked at her and the galaxies in his eyes had dimmed so much that the only light in them now came from the event horizon of the supermassive black holes in their centres. This was more than just wrong, it was disastrous.

"I'm sorry, Maggie." He bit his lip and looked down. "I don't know why, but I can't heal you."

"You can, you have to."

"I can't. I'm sure it's just temporary, but right now, I can't help you." He turned to Enzo. "She'll need first aid, and someone has to check for internal injuries. Can one of your people do that?"

"You have to." She grabbed Nico's shoulders, buried her fingers into his stuffing. "You can heal me, I know you can."

"I can't right now," he replied. "I'm sorry. It isn't working."

It didn't make sense. She'd made a wish and it had been granted. She'd been super specific too, just like the origin demanded, because she'd been paying attention when he spoke about how the Apocalypse was caused by people being vague on the details. She'd covered everything, hadn't she?

The terms and conditions. The shadow man warned her they governed everything. What had he said? Causes and effects had to balance and you didn't hold the hand that punched you. She'd changed Nico's power without his permission and this was the result: Nico couldn't heal her at all.

Maggie burned and shrivelled. Pus oozed up from beneath the mould and erupted from gaps between the stitches, coating her skin, making her hand stick to the railing when she started down the stairs. The movie poster with Rob's face mocked her from its place on the wall. She hadn't seen the ending so she'd made something up, tried to make something good for herself. She'd been so careful to make sure Nico could heal any mental ailments, and all for nothing because she didn't ask first.

It was fucking unfair. Why should she suffer when she'd done him a favour?

Maggie missed a step and fell to her knees on the landing. Mud splattered onto her thighs and squelched coldly against her skin. If she wanted to gain entrance to that frolicking place where all the normal people were then she needed to find the origin and make him make it all right.

"Do I have to drag you out of here?"

Maggie looked up into Luan's gun and the catfish bit through the membrane that had held them imprisoned. They were laughing at her. Mud leaked from their gaping mouths and their tails slapped at the boxes she hadn't had time to tidy up yet. One of them reached for the gun and another bit at the straw poking from the scarecrow's sleeve. Luan's eyes grew big, bursting from their sockets to orbit his head and Maggie wondered if he could still see through them.

The catfish were swarming his feet now, mouths gaping and whiskers writhing. She took several of the chains draped over a hook in the wall, attached them to the catfishes' collars and dragged them away. It was time she got rid of them forever.

Bottom-feeder

"Bravely, Maggie marched towards the place where her better self was taken from her. She ignored her fear and the growing certainty that she was on the verge of a precipice in her sanity from which she might never return."

The narrator was just a step behind her, his strides in sync with hers, his purple cloak sweeping through the weeds and overgrown grass. The catfish swam through the green as they would in water but her and the narrator's trails twinned like railway tracks from the spot where she stepped off the bridge to the Loch Logan island.

"You look stupid dressed like that," she said. "Who wears a cloak outside of a cosplay con?"

The narrator smiled. "She was determined to do the right thing, even if she wasn't entirely certain what that was or how she might define it. Her instincts would be her guide, she thought, because they had read the script, unlike her."

Maggie walked faster, tugging on the catfish so they'd keep up. "I would've read the script if someone had given it to me."

"This was not the first lie Maggie told, but it would prove to be the last. She didn't know it yet, but she wouldn't walk away from—"

"Shut up!" Maggie spun on the narrator and whipped him with the ends of the chains attached to the catfish.

His cloak opened into petals around him as he spun, arms spreading to invite hugs before he fell to one knee. The long grass lifted ribbons to catch him, which cradled him, straightened him and wove into a basket around him.

"I'm very sorry, but I can't care about these sideways things any more, okay? I'm done with people and their issues with me, and I'm done with all the things they want me to be for them. And that includes you." She jabbed her finger at the narrator. "Stop trying to make me fit into your story."

"The cinematographer takes a moment to shine at this point, panning out to render the scene from a distance before zooming in on the light strobing off the catfishes' wet skin as they writhe in grass painted electric colours." The narrator used the rim of the basket to sit up and spat out a mouthful of blood over the side. "It's dramatic because it's the beginning of a terrible—"

"Stop it!" Maggie combed the grass for the basket's lid. "I'm not going to listen to you. I'm never going to be your version of me."

"—transformation, because now Maggie knows she's still in a movie and that it's been a movie all along. She never left the water and the willow tree." He looked up at her with Arno's eyes and Arno's teeth biting Arno's lower lip. "She's been with me all along. I've been inside her all along."

"You're a fucking liar." Maggie found the lid and slammed it down over the narrator, silencing him. "And even if it is a movie, it's my movie, and I'll decide what happens in it."

"She can't do that!" The lid pressed up against her hand as the narrator fought for freedom. "I made the catfish and the TV. I made her. Nobody can take Maggie from me!"

"I can."

Maggie punched the lid until it was still. She then transferred all the chains to one hand so she could grasp the handle on the basket with the other, adding it to her burdens as she continued towards the river.

"I'm writing the script now. I'm also the producer, and the director. Yes." She nodded to herself. For too long she'd been confined in storylines that normal people imposed on her. In the realest of realities she wouldn't need to hunt down some double-crossing bogeyman so she could be better, so she could be accepted. For other reasons maybe, but not that. So she'd make a different story, a story where things were nice. She just needed to tidy up first.

Maggie stepped onto the line where the ground sloped away down to the shallow river. The catfish were waiting for her, dark slicks with gaping mouths foaming the water with their tails and forcing the Egyptian geese to walk across their backs to reach open water. She lifted the lid off the basket and kicked it down the bank. It tumbled and rolled, flattening a path, dressing the catfish in the narrator's empty skin and cloak. He must've left without her noticing, but it didn't matter because she was going to fire him anyway.

Maggie didn't follow the skin yet. The catfish strained at their chains when Maggie led them to one of the brick and concrete braai altars that had been placed on the island in more pallid times. She tied them to a tree and cleared away the old plastic bags and leaves and semi-rotted masks on one of the benches. There was a knife and a hand buried beneath the weeds, archaeological evidence of the meat worship that once occurred here. Maggie wiped the blade off on her shirt and lifted the first catfish onto the bench. She was missing many of the holy sacraments—there was no fire or firestarters, no tongs and no spice—but her instincts told her that this was the place to kill her demons.

They wriggled and slithered, they slipped and slapped, but one by one she took the catfishes' heads and opened their hearts to the sun and shadows. She laid each one into the basket lid when she was finished, and when she was finished with being finished, it was sunset. Maggie lifted her hands to the sky and watched the blood from the catfish dribble down her fingers. It was red like weaver birds, her fingers straight as feathers. Fortune-cookie wisdoms glittered around her but they were too quick on the air for her to read what they said and it didn't matter. It was better to watch them fly, to catch them and press them into her skin where they could bandage the pus and mould.

Her sacrificial catfish were greedily accepted by the catfish dressed in the narrator's cloak. Maggie didn't watch the cannibalism. Instead, she washed her hands and set to tidying the boxes that had tumbled about in her head since the origin shook her thoughts. She packed away the movie posters and added chlorine to the mud at the bottom of the water slides. It wasn't as good as Nico's starlight but it would do for now. The stitches and seams would be inaccessible until the pus and fortune-cookie papers formed scabs but she put a thread unpicker in her pocket so she could deal with them later. Now, she was ready.

She placed a billboard over the top of the water slides so all the thoughts and mould and stitches would have access to the script. No. A storyboard would be better, more attention grabbing and therefore not as easy to ignore as lines of words.

She painted herself returning to the zoo in cyan and yellow. There, she found Rob and Nico outside the hotel, waiting for her. Both of them were navy blue. Rob would put his hands on her shoulders and Nico would spout apologies about everything, and it would all be genuine because they were going to care about her for real and who she really was. She'd nod and tell them she was okay and take them to where she left Freddy because one part needed to end before a new one could begin.

Freddy would be orange when they all reunited, and it would be awkward so she skipped over that part for now. She'd convince them that they needed to test Nico's power, and then she'd have to catch someone like her so they could do that. Freddy hunted with her in the next scene, his orange a little too close to brown to work with her cyan and yellow, but it would change over time as they caught more crazies for Nico to heal. Rob would support the idea, and support her, and they'd all bond into a happy home while they helped as many people like her as they could.

Travelling would happen while they did that because they'd be chasing the origin too. They'd have to. He had tricked her, and that trick turned into pins that popped her balloon. They'd find him in Joburg, just like Rob said they would, and everything would be magenta. She'd force him to change his terms and conditions and then, finally, Nico would heal her. She would shine then, and her balloon would return to her chest. There'd be tears and confetti, hugs and laughter. All the people like her who she and Freddy had caught for Nico to heal would be there too because it was the happily ever after. They'd watch her present her sanity ticket to the bouncer, and everyone would cheer when she was allowed into the frolicking place with them.

Maggie flicked back to the beginning of the storyboard and flipped through it again and again. She paused to add a scene where she saved Freddy's life so he could give her his horns as a sign of his gratitude afterwards, and a scene where she squished Nico until his stuffing burst from his nose, and a scene where Rob parted his skin for her so she could see the light inside his head.

She added puppies and a party, gardens filled with ripe tomatoes, and cold rain that made it easier to sleep during hot afternoons. All good things went into the storyboard. When it felt like she'd done enough to make up for all the sadness and suffering she'd endured so far, Maggie added an ending where the origin took away the shadows but left their powers. Last of all, she gave it a title: How to Save the World.

Acknowledgments

My thanks go out to A, whose professional insight into psychosis helped me evoke the unreality as authentically as possible, despite the need to take artistic liberties. Also to my agent, Bieke, and coach, Martijn. Thanks for giving this weird story a shot.

To Gio, who is both an amazing friend and valued critique partner. As always, this story wouldn't be quite the same without you.

Discover Luna Novella in our store:

https://www.lunapresspublishing.com/shop

Milton Keynes UK
Ingram Content Group UK Ltd.
UKHW021610070124
435586UK00004B/250

9 781915 556226